THE
SNOWFLAKE

GEORGE TURELL

WORKBOOK PRESS LLC
187 E Warm Springs Rd,
Suite B285, Las Vegas, NV 89119, USA

Website: https://workbookpress.com/
Hotline: 1-888-818-4856
Email: admin@workbookpress.com

Ordering Information:
Quantity sales. Special discounts are available on quantity purchases by corporations, associations, and others. For details, contact the publisher at the address above.

ISBN-13:   978-1-954753-05-1 (Paperback Version)
                      978-1-954753-06-8 (Digital Version)

REV. DATE: 26.01.2021

TABLE OF CONTENTS

I

THE NEW ADVENTURE

NOW, I HAVE MADE MY decision. 'The rice is cooked', as the Chinese say. Yesterday I wrote my letter of resignation to Commercial Chemicals, where I had worked for the past three years. I had hoped to develop fundamental research on the structure of polymer films. In spite of my efforts, the Administration decided to put all of its emphasis — and budget — on the development of 'better meat-wraps'. It was the obvious end of any fundamental scientific work in the Research Center.

And then, I wrote a letter to Haywood University in DC to accept their offer of an Associate Professorship in Physical Chemistry. All I could hope for was that the academic atmosphere would be more compatible with my ideas of scientific research. Clearly, with the added task of full-time teaching and, most certainly, a limited budget for research, I was taking a chance. As for the practical side, I had to organize a move to Washington.

Before leaving I made a last visit to the Center. I had no friends there, although I had much appreciated the work with Alan, my technician. I saw him briefly. We spoke of Ben and his demise — what a tragic affaire! He had committed suicide. It could not have been only due to the changes in the Administration of the Center, we thought. In fact, I had guessed that he had personal problems, as well as certain difficulties to continue his music in this area. I said 'goodbye' to Alan and promised to keep in contact. I didn't see Nina, the mail girl, with whom I had had one fabulous night out. She was difficult to forget, but it was obvious that she was not interested in the 'intellectual society', as she put it and, above all, was not willing to move 'down South' to Washington. Too bad — maybe.

The old Ford was still acting up. I managed to get it over to the garage, where the mechanic saw me coming. He knew the car well and when I asked about its future, he only shook his head. He then remarked,

"If you're interested in buying another car, I can show you several that are in good condition. Your poor Ford has had a long, tough life. It's true that it has four new tires, so I can offer you $50 toward a newer car." I replied that I'd have to think about it, as I was planning to move to Washington. "Oh, what are you going to do down there," he asked? I explained that I had accepted a university job. "I'll bet you'll earn a lot less money than you've been getting at the Center," he remarked. "Yes, that is quite true, but I hope for more freedom to do what I want to do." Clearly my argument was not very convincing — maybe not to me either.

I took a bus back to my apartment and started packing. I was still worrying about the car. After some thought, I decided to let the question drop until I was settled in DC. All would depend on where I was located in the city and transportation to-and-from the university. I had visited Washington several years before and, as I remembered, public transportation was very good and taxis were quite cheap. I put all of my belongings in several footlockers and called a moving company to pick them up, along with the few pieces of furniture that I had bought for my studio. I gave my university address, but insisted that all be put 'on hold' until I had found an apartment in Washington. I left my little place in New Jersey with a big suitcase of my immediate needs.

I took the train in Newark. It made a quick stop at Princeton Junction and then continued. I thought of my previous visits to Princeton, the well-known university, where I was a couple of years ago invited to give a seminar. The next stop was for Trenton, the capital of New Jersey. It was nevertheless, primarily a jumping-off point for Atlantic City. At that center of anti-culture, I had participated in the 'Instrument Show', the presentation of scientific apparatus of all kinds. Of course I had visited the Casino. No comment and nothing won.

Next, there was a brief stop at North Philadelphia before going up to cross the Schuylkill River. I looked out to see Fairmont Park and the Philadelphia Zoo. The train then turned down along the river to the 30th Street Station. Here, we stayed a bit longer, and, as we were pulling out of the station, another passenger arrived. He stopped next to my place and addressed me with, "Good afternoon, Sir, is this seat taken?" I was surprised by his politeness. I responded, "No, not at all, please take this place," as I indicated the seat next to me.

He was tall, probably still in his twenties, and somewhat dark. My mother would have described him as 'café au lait'. She would certainly have said that he was a 'handsome guy'. I started the conversation with the usual traveler's question: "How far are you going, on to Washington?" He replied, "Yes, that's right, I live down there." He went on to explain that his parents were from Philadelphia — 'Philly', as he called it, and that he was studying in Washington. "And so," I asked, "What are you studying? Are you at a university there?" He then explained that he was a medical student, with another two years to finish his degree. In the meantime, at night, he was earning his living as a taxi driver in Washington. "But how do you have the energy to do all that; when do you sleep," I asked? "Well, it isn't always easy, but soon I hope to be an MD. Then I'll be able to establish myself and earn my way more normally."

He then turned to me and asked, "And what do you do?" He had obviously learned about the art of conversation. (After a dialogue, one should ask himself: "Who learned more?" If it was the other person, you talked too much!) I answered with, "I'm originally from Massachusetts, a small town that is almost entirely French-speaking. I did my graduate work at Brown University and then took a job with Commercial Chemicals in New Jersey. There, at the Research Center I tried to develop fundamental studies of plastics, primarily with the use of optical methods. Unfortunately, the management didn't appreciate my efforts and I resigned to accept a teaching and research post in chemistry at Haywood University."

My companion was obviously startled, but then replied, "I am honored to make your acquaintance, Professor, my name is Jim Hawkins. My medical school is part of Haywood University and my training in chemistry was in the Department there." I extended my hand and introduced myself; "I'm Jack Gilbert. It is indeed a pleasure to meet you, Jim, my first personal contact with the University."

As the train slowed down for the stop in Wilmington, we saw the famous two tall buildings. "Oh yes", I remarked, "Here we are in 'plasticland', the home of Uncle Dupy. The researchers here were our major competitors when I was at the Center in New Jersey. It seems that one of their principal interests is PTFE, polytetrafluoroethylene. They are now considering its use as a coating for pots and pans." Jim immediately responded with, "But the fluorocarbons are very dangerous at high temperatures; how can they be used in cooking?" "You are quite right and, in fact, it is just for that reason the company here has not yet put their 'nonstick' pans on the market. They have to prove that there is no danger to the consumer, at least at temperatures up to 300° centigrade or so."

As we left Wilmington for the long haul down to Baltimore, I understood that my friend was very tired. I stopped talking and saw that he was soon fast asleep — no wonder, considering the hectic life he was leading.

I started thinking of the future. I was most impressed by Jim. If he was typical of students at Haywood, I could expect to have a very interesting and rewarding position there. As for my part, I realized that I had had little or no teaching experience. Research, OK, but I would certainly have to work hard to develop classroom techniques and the necessary self confidence.

Jim woke up with the call for Baltimore. He then told me a little about the history of Haywood University. "It was founded several years after the Civil War to offer the possibility of higher education to Negroes — the 'freed' slaves — as they were not allowed to enter the so-called 'white' universities. Haywood was created by the Federal Government, which is still its major source of finances. It is thus the only truly Federal University in the United States. By the way, the University is not uniquely for Negroes, as it is open to all. However, some 80% of its student body is composed of what my grandmother calls, "Us cullèd foks". The rest are primarily of Indian or Pakistani origin, as well as a significant number from the Middle East. The number of WASP's is negligible."

I hesitated, and Jim understood. "Well, you know (although I didn't), the abbreviation WASP is used for 'White, Anglo-Saxon Protestants'. It's really not intended to be offensive — just our way of describing a certain, most important cross-section of the American population. By the way the correct description of us is 'Negro', and the race, as Negroid. However, it has now fallen into disuse by the younger generation, who prefer 'Black'.

Clearly, this question is without meaning, unless you have a preference for Spanish or English — and obviously neither black nor white is a very accurate description of skin color."

I thanked Jim for his interesting history of the University an his remarks on the American Society. As we approached Washington, we could see the Capitol in the distance. Jim stood up and took down his little suitcase. He remarked that he would have to get a bite to eat before venturing out in his taxi for the night. I reminded Jim that I would soon have an office in the Chemistry building and added, "Please don't hesitate to stop by; I would like to keep in touch." We said our 'goodbyes' and shook hands. The train stopped in Union Station. It was the end of the trip and, for me, the beginning of a new adventure.

THE NATION'S CAPITAL

I WAS ON THE PLATFORM AT Union Station in DC. I walked down and entered the huge waiting room. I had no other baggage, just my suitcase that I checked in a locker. I was glad that I had arranged to send all the rest of my stuff. On the other side of the station I stepped out into the brilliant sunshine. It was terribly humid — suffocating. The big fountain was invaded by little Negro children enjoying the relief from the hot weather. In the background I could see the Senate Office Building and, just behind, the dome of the Capitol.

I headed down to Constitution Avenue and followed The Mall, with the Washington Monument in the distance. As I passed in front of the National Gallery, I thought back to the last time I visited Washington. It was with Allison, my girlfriend when I was a graduate student in Providence. She was at the art school there, so insisted on a visit to Washington — especially to see the National Gallery and the Phillips Collection. I often missed her, but she was definitely too 'arty' for me. At seventh street I took the trolley — or was it called a 'street car'?

I noticed that there were several dark-skinned persons in the car and was reminded of what someone had told me, that public transportation in Washington had only very recently been desegregated. How was it possible? It had been almost a century since Lincoln had signed the Emancipation Proclamation, and was it only just now that some results were to be seen? As we continued North on seventh avenue, the white passengers began to get off and the 'colored', as Jim had called them, began to enter. We stopped at O street, the market. Most of the 'whites' got off to take the cross-town bus toward Georgetown. From there on it was Georgia Avenue, lined with boarded-up shops and litter on the street. By the time we got to Florida Avenue I realized that I was the only snowflake in the street car.

At Haywood place I got off and walked up the hill to the University campus. I was impressed by the architecture of the various buildings. It was apparent that several dated from the past century, although many were very modern. I stopped a student to inquire: "Please, I'm looking for the Chemistry building." He replied, "Yes, Sir, just continue up the hill towards the library; it's the big building that you see up there. Then, just down to your right there is a building with big Doric columns; that's Chemistry." I thanked him for the information and continued up the hill. I thought, "Doric columns?" He certainly knew something of Greek architecture.

I went into the building and saw the Chemistry Department office on the right. I entered and asked if I could see the Department Chairman. The secretary was a fair-skinned lady who asked if I had an appointment. (I learned later that she was always called Mrs. Jones). I replied, "Oh no, but I wrote to Dr. Fillmore to say that I would come in today. My name is Jack Gilbert. I'm the new member of the chemistry faculty." She leaped up and went running into the office behind. "Dr. Fillmore, the new teacher has arrived!" He came out immediately to greet me, with, "I am pleased to meet you, Dr. Gilbert, and we are indeed honored that you have come to join us." He was tall, fairly dark and built to be a football player.

He began immediately to arrange my arrival at the University. He asked, "Have you found a place to stay?" "No," I replied, "It will probably be a few days before my things arrive from New Jersey. My suitcase is at Union Station." "OK, Mrs. Jones will telephone to reserve a room for you. I suggest that you take a place at one of the tourist homes along south C street. That's quite near the Capitol and convenient for you to go there with your suitcase. Once you are established, Mrs. Jones can help you find a better lodging. By the way, I rather assumed that you didn't drive down to Washington." "No," I replied, "I sold my old car before leaving New Jersey, so I am, as the Brown boys say, 'without wheels'." I suddenly had a sinking feeling. I had referred to the 'Brown boys', meaning the students at Brown University, without any thought of the local implication. Dr. Fillmore responded without a hitch, "Yes, of course, but public transportation here in Washington is now very good, and even available to everyone."

I was impressed by Dr. Fillmore's understanding, and his organization. I thought, "If he is like that as Head of the Department, it should function very well." He then led me across the hall, where he opened the door to an office. He said, "This is your new office; we hope that you will find it satisfactory." It was perfect. There was a window toward the lower campus — the schools of medicine and dentistry. There was a big desk, a filing cabinet and two bookcases that I would soon be able to fill with the many books that I had collected during the past ten years or so.

I left the University campus with a feeling of satisfaction with my choice of the position and enthusiasm for the prospect of continuing scientific research. Dr. Fillmore had assured me that I could have all the lab space I would need, although the financial aid from the Department would be somewhat limited. It was obvious that I would have to look for research money in the form of contracts from the 'outside'.

Again on the streetcar, I descended into the tourist center of DC. Mrs. Jones had given me the address on C street, where she had reserved a room for me. At the Mall I saw again the National Gallery on the left and, in the distance on the right, the old building of the Smithsonian Museum. I got off on Independence Avenue and started up toward the Capitol. At Pennsylvania Avenue I turned down to C street and continued a couple of blocks further to the address that Mrs. Jones had given me. At the tourist home I was welcomed by a middle-aged lady who said that my room had been reserved. I explained that my suitcase was at the Station, so I would go after it and return shortly.

I walked back along C street and turned north toward the Union Station, with the Library of Congress on my right and the Capitol on my left. I then understood that Washington, DC, is a center of information, of culture, and history. Museums and archives that are unique in the World can be found there. I was very impressed and decided that I would certainly profit from what this city had to offer.

At Union Station I found my suitcase in the locker and lugged it out into the sunshine. I hailed a taxi and was in five minutes back at the tourist home.

The next day Mrs. Jones phoned me to ask if I would like to look at an apartment. She explained that it was straight north from the campus, up Georgia Avenue, not more than ten minutes on the streetcar. I went by the Department to pick up the key and got back on the streetcar. I took one look at the apartment and decided that it was just what I needed.

I took the occasion to look around the neighborhood. It was a sort of no-man's land — or better, perhaps — an 'every-bodies land'. South, the area around the University was entirely populated by 'blacks'. I soon learned that further north, near the Maryland border, it was mostly WASPs — to use the expression that Jim had taught me. There were also a few Jews, but no blacks. Near my new apartment, within a few blocks, I found a Greek grocery store, a Jewish delicatessen and an Italian market. There were also two restaurants, one Chinese and one Italian. I was very happy with 'my' new neighborhood.

The next day I went for a walk over to 14th street, where I found a drug store. On the way I passed a big house that had been converted into a Negro Baptist church. The door was open and Gospel singing came out — loud, and with much rhythm. The singing was accompanied by handclapping and a tambourine or two. In spite of my curiosity, I didn't go in for fear of being unwelcome.

I bought a paperback best-seller at the corner drug store and wandered back along another route. I passed two little colored boys playing in front of a big frame house. I heard one of them say, "Let's go'n playin, but dis tym you'll be deh Injin an ahm gona be deh white man."

A few days later I received all my stuff from New Jersey and arranged my little studio without too much effort. However, it was down at the University where my work would be more difficult. Teaching was a new experience for me.

ACADEMIA

AT THE LAB I HAD soon arranged my office. The bookcases were now filled and I began to make the acquaintance of my colleagues. Dr. Fillmore introduced me to Mr. Watson, whom he described as, "The person who does everything around here." I soon found that the description of Mr. Watson was correct. He gave me the various keys and came to my office to be sure that everything was as needed. I did ask him if I could have a blackboard on the wall, to which he responded, "But of course."

That afternoon a technician came, a certain Mr. Lavigne, to put up the blackboard. We chatted a bit and I asked him if, with the family name Lavigne, he spoke French. He laughed and replied, "Not at all, in fact I doubt if I have any French ancestors. You may not realize that at the time we Negroes were freed, a hundred years ago, we had little or no family structure, and hence no family names. We were always called by our first names and, when freed, usually took the name of the former slave owner. In my case he was apparently of French origin."

It was true that I had never thought about the question, but I had noticed that within the Department, there was a definite formality. First names were rarely used, even among colleagues, and the titles Miss. or Mrs., Mr. or Dr., were invariably respected. I noticed also that there were no female faculty members.

I soon became accustomed to life in the Department and gradually accepted being called "Dr. Gilbert". I was asked to teach two courses, one at a graduate level. Clearly, it would require a lot of preparation. In addition, I had the responsibility for organizing the Physical Chemistry laboratory and advising new students. The latter task was very interesting, but difficult, as I didn't know the course program at the University. However, little-by-little I learned and it was an opportunity to meet the incoming undergraduate students. I had to admit the some had accents that were difficult to understand.

One evening I had stayed very late in my office. In fact it was already dark when I came down the hill to take the street car. A student was waiting there on the corner when a voice came down out of the darkness. It asked, "Hoo dat dhair?" The student next to me returned the question with, "Hoo dat say hoo dat?" Yes, it was a different language. I was told that 'black English' was now being taught in the DC public schools.

As for my colleagues, I had only met a few of them. One morning I crossed Dr. Fillmore in the hall. He asked me If I had met Dr. Savinski. I replied that I had not had the pleasure. The Director went on to explain that Dr. Savinski was the senior member of the Chemistry Faculty. "He will be retiring at the end of this Academic Year. If you're not busy at lunchtime, would you like to join us?" "But yes, I would be honored." I replied. We agreed to met in Dr. Fillmore's office at noon.

Dr. Savinski was short, wore rimless glasses and was mostly bald. His fringe of grey hair was quite long. He was certainly of Jewish, Central European origin. He explained that he came into the Department almost forty years earlier and described himself as, "The first more-or-less white member of the Faculty."

We went down to the parking lot, where Dr. Fillmore stopped beside a big French car — A Citroën DS. I was quite surprised to see it, and asked, "How do you happen to have this car? They are very rare here." He laughed, and answered that he had been in Europe for his Sabbatical and had brought the car back with him." He added, "I refused to buy a German car; you probably understand." He remarked that the only problem with the DS was repairs, as few mechanics were familiar with it and parts were hard to find.

Dr. Fillmore drove us to the Washington Hospital Center. I may have looked a bit puzzled, as he explained. "In spite of much progress in integration, it is still very difficult to find a restaurant that will accept racially mixed groups." I said that I was astonished that segregation still existed, but Dr. Fillmore pointed out that not only was it the dominant situation, but that it was applied in both white and black establishments. The exceptions were Government Institutions, such as the Hospital

Center, where the anti-segregation laws were applied — and respected.

At the lunch table, we talked of the rather special society of the DC area. It was evident that the Federal Government plays the dominant role there. He described the flux in the population, as the majority party often changed after an election. He also confirmed what Jim had told me on the train, that Haywood University, as a Federal Institution, was unique in the United States. He spoke briefly of some Departmental matters and remarked that there would be a faculty meeting in a few days. "It will give you, Dr. Gilbert, your first chance to meet all of your colleagues — and for them to see you!"

At the meeting the following week, I was introduced as the new member of the Chemistry faculty. Dr. Fillmore gave a short résumé of my background and received an applause from the group. I noticed that I was the tenth teacher in the Department and, as if by chance, there were five darker-skinned members of the group and five of us snowflakes. I was told afterwards that there had been a systematic effort to maintain the racial balance.

Dr. Fillmore presided over the meeting with precision. He presented each subject to be considered and allowed time for comments and discussion — following "Robert's Rules of Order". All was timed with a stopwatch. He brought up the important question of the research budget and suggested that I be accorded a bit extra this year, as it was my first. However, he made it quite clear that to do serious research I would have to get grants from outside the University. It was agreed that to help me get started the Department would finance the purchase of a commercial infrared spectrometer, as it was of general interest, and in particular mine. I thanked the group for their support.

Near the end of the year I was sitting at my desk, thinking through my next lecture, when there was a tap and a tall figure appeared in the open doorway. It was Jim, whom I had met on the train down to Washington. "Oh, hello, Jim, thanks for coming by. Please come in and tell me how your studies are going." He came in, extending his hand, and said, "Dr. Gilbert, it's good to see you. You appear to be settled into your new office."

"Yes", I replied, "And I am pleased with the atmosphere of the Department. It has taken me a bit of time to get used to preparing lectures, but I'm now happy with the results. And, what about you? You should be seeing the end of your long program at the Medical School."

"You are quite right, Dr. Gilbert, but I still have some work to do. To be honest, that's one of the reasons for my visit today. I hope that you can help me." "Of course, what can I do," I asked? Jim continued, "In the last year of the program we are required to present the results of a little research project. Of course it is expected to be somewhat oriented toward medicine. I thought that you, as a spectroscopist, might have some suggestions."

My first thought was of the new infrared machine. "Well, Jim, I think that you could try to get infrared spectra of a molecule or two of biological interest. Many are pharmaceuticals, whose drug activity depends on the orientation of certain functional groups. You should be able to detect this effect from their infrared spectra." "But that's great," he responded; "Please explain how to do the experiments."

"OK, let's go down to see the new spectrometer. I'll show you how it works— and what is much more difficult — give you some idea of how to interpret the results." We went into the big lab, where the new instrument was on display. Several of my colleagues had come in to look at it and to inquire about its chemical applications.

I picked up a piece of chart paper that presented the spectrum of polyethylene. The tracing looked very much like a mountain range. I explained that it was the usual test sample for the instrument. It showed the absorption of various wavelengths of light in the infrared region of the spectrum. "Here," I indicated, "Is the region that is characteristic of hydrogen atoms — nothing new, as we know that they are present in this compound. However, down here in this region we see certain peaks that indicate immediately that the benzene ring is mono-substituted. A detailed analysis would provide additional information about the structure of this molecule."

I could feel the excitement as Jim exclaimed, "But this is fascinating! Tell me how to put other samples, powders, for example, in the machine."

I replied, "You have just asked a good question. Sample preparation is certainly one of the more difficult problems in infrared spectroscopy. I'll give you some lessons once you are established. Here, come along with me," as I opened the door to a small office. "You can use this room while you're working on your project. Just now it's not occupied, although I'm hoping to have a postdoc here next year."

Jim thanked me profusely for the demonstration and the invitation to use the office. He said that he would spend a week or so reading up on infrared spectroscopy, and that he would then come by for some help with the experiments.

From time-to-time a first-year graduate student would come to my office to ask about my research. Each was looking for an interesting — and hopefully successful — project for a Masters thesis. Sometimes it was a more advanced student working on the M.S. with one of my colleagues. In this case it was a question of research for the Doctorate, the most important questions being the possibility of a stipend, the time that might be needed to complete the project and, of course, its feasibility. These questions were invariably related to his family responsibilities. Furthermore, for him to become a doctoral candidate, he would have to pass the preliminary examinations — the 'prelims' — in several branches of Chemistry.

In the course of the next two semesters, I was able to obtain funding for my research from various sources. The budget then allowed me to offer stipends to several graduate students and perhaps a 'postdoc'.

Jim was able to get spectra of several molecules of biological interest. He wrote up his results to show me and presented the document at the medical school. After the ceremony at which he was awarded the doctor's degree, he came to see me. I stood up to shake hands and offer my congratulations.

When I asked Jim about his future plans, he hesitated. "You know," he said, "I've been thinking a lot. I have been strongly motivated by my research experience here in your group. I think that I would prefer go into medical research, rather than practicing. What do you think?" I replied, "But Jim, I'm really not in a position to advise you. However, it is apparent that to start practice involves a considerable investment, unless you can find an established physician who is willing to take you on as a partner. A research post would certainly not earn you as much money, although it would be more stable and probably involve less risk. Why don't you think about it for a couple of days and come back to see me?" Jim left with another handshake and a somewhat worried look.

When Jim returned he announced, "I have reached a decision. I want to continue in research. I need two or three years of experience before I can hope to have a post in one of the medical research establishments. There are several in the region." I replied with my proposal. "Jim, I now have enough research money to pay a postdoc. Would you be willing to accept the job?" He answered immediately with, "Yes indeed, I had hoped for such an offer." I explained that the salary would not be very high, but certainly would allow him to give up his taxi outings. I indicated that his salary could start the first of the following month and that I would trust him with the responsibility for the infrared machine. Jim seemed very happy with the arrangement.

On the personal side, with the research contracts I could pay myself to continue research during the summer months. Otherwise, I had to teach Summer School or look for a three-months job. The research contracts usually included a certain budget for travel, for seminars and scientific meetings. Thus, I had enough money to attend my first Gordon Conference.

These Conferences were weeklong meetings of a selected group of scientists in a given, very specialized field of research. I received the list of the participants for the meeting on vibrational spectroscopy and found that my request to attend had been accepted. There were sixty or so on the list, including a dozen great names in the field.

I took the train in Washington for the trip up north. Baltimore, Philadelphia, New York, Albany — It was an all-day trip into New England. I was born over there, just east, but I had not been back since the death of my mother several years ago. My father had died much earlier, so I had no more relatives in that part of the world. I got off when the train stopped for a couple of minutes in Burlington, Vermont. I crossed the platform with my little suitcase and saw a minibus, with a sign on the windshield: "Gordon Conferences". The driver was standing there awaiting those scientists arriving by train.

A boarding school was rented for the summer series of conferences and the participants were lodged in what was the residence hall for the boys during the school year. Each morning was devoted to lectures by invited scientists — followed by discussions. In the evening, after dinner the lectures continued, leaving the afternoons free for other activities — hiking, tennis, … and for a few who had stayed up too late discussing (and drinking) it was the time for siestas.

One afternoon I was walking along a path through the woods when I heard a group arriving. There were four of them speaking French. I recognized Mlle. Josik, as she had given a talk that morning. She was a middle-aged lady, who had been introduced as a Professor at the Sorbonne. She was still addressed as 'Mademoiselle' in spite of her age. It was the honor of her stature that took precedence over the French tradition. The members of the little hiking group were amazed when I greeted them in French.

During the week of the meeting, I became better acquainted with Mlle. Josik. I explained my origin and apologized for my infantile French, as it was only as a child that I had spoken it. She replied that it was quite understandable and that if I were to come to France for a visit, it would very rapidly improve. She said, "All you have to do is develop your technical vocabulary. But after all, most scientific words have Latin roots and are thus the same in English and French."

I returned to Washington after a very enjoyable experience at the Gordon Conference. I had only been in my office a few minutes when there was a tap at the door and Mr. Watson came in with, "Hello, Dr. Gilbert, welcome back. Did you have a good trip?" "In fact it was extraordinary." I responded, "It was a very enriching experience, not only because of the science, but also from a cultural point of view. I met several of the most important people in my field of research. They came from all parts of the World. Although all at the Conference was in English, I did have the occasion to speak French with several of the other participants. I most certainly made contacts with other researchers in spectroscopy. "And, so, how has it been going back here, Mr. Watson?"

"Back here? Well, that's another story. There has been a very strange incident. One day last week one of our young students was going into the General Chemistry Laboratory, when she touched the doorknob at the entrance. She immediately felt a burning sensation on her hand and came running down to my office. I took her quickly into the lab down the hall and rinsed her hand in dilute ammonia. She was immediately relieved and has not shown any signs of burns. However the question remained as to the origin of the acid on the doorknob."

Mr. Watson continued, "That evening, when the graduate students had left the building, I did a little detective work. I have a master key, of course. So, I went upstairs to take a look at each little research lab. In one of them, it was Morton James' lab, I found a beaker of sulfuric acid and an old paintbrush. Of course that's not proof that he painted the acid on the doorknob in question, as it could have been planted by another person. However, it is sufficient to suggest that we watch the 'little wart'. He could be very dangerous."

I was, to say the least, startled by this story. I responded to Mr. Watson with, "Are you not, in fact, in detective work? I would say that you did a good job there. But it's not obvious that we can do more than to keep an eye on that little guy."

MARGO

I HAD BEEN TEACHING THE UNDERGRADUATE physical chemistry class for two years now. In the Fall there was always a new batch of thirty or so students. I had really not noticed them, although I was attracted by some of the relatively few young ladies. I had to admit that I was not accustomed to the racial differences, as I had been brought up in New England. The negroïds, as a description of their racial background, just didn't have the same morphology. I found that the evaluation, or even the appreciation, was a question of the society — the immediate environment. And so, I felt that I was becoming integrated into the University community. In fact, one day a colleague made the remark, "But now you are an honorary 'black'." I was very pleased.

Among the students, in particular, one of the young ones was unusually attractive. It was during the mid-term exam when I had the time to look over the class — in principle to be sure that nobody was cheating. I tried to avoid looking too often at the young person in question. I knew that her name was Margo, but we had never spoken. She was short, a bit round — some of my fellow students way back when would have described her as 'comfortable' — easy to imagine. I tried to think of other things until I collected the exam papers at the end of the hour.

Back in my apartment that afternoon, I corrected the stack of papers. Margo's effort was far from satisfactory, well below the average. Too bad, I thought, but nothing to do with her looks, or my imagination.

The next morning, after my lecture to the graduate students, I was in my office when there was a timid tap at the door. With my "Come in," Margo did so and closed the door behind her. I stood up, as she came towards me with tears in her big brown eyes. "I just had to see you, Dr. Gilbert, because I'm so ashamed. I don't know how I could have done so badly on your mid-term." I replied, "Yes, it's true, you didn't do well this time. But, don't worry about it; if you study, you'll do better on the final. If you need help, don't hesitate to come by."

After my class the following morning she came again to my office. This time there were no tears. She came in with a somewhat suggestive body movement. She approached and pressed her full breasts against me and with a little kiss on my neck, laid her head on my shoulder. There was no way to resist. I responded, "Please be careful, we can't do anything here." "But where," she asked? "Unless I can come to your place. I know where it is: number 674 on Madison, in the third alphabet. I live very near, with my parents on Colorado Avenue." "How did you know my address," I asked? She answered, "I can read the telephone book, even if I'm not any good at physical chemistry."

I had to hesitate. But, after all, what could any young man do under the circumstances? Nothing. "This afternoon, she asked?" "Oh, yes," I responded, "See you then." She danced out with her provocative body and a knowing smile.

That afternoon I tried to concentrate. It was difficult. I looked around my little bachelor apartment and started picking up a bit. Then I thought of the bed! If we were to get that far, it would have to be — to say the least — acceptable. I changed the sheets and remade the bed. Yes, I was looking forward to an adventure that I had overlooked for too long now.

A bit later there was a ring from the entrance to the building. I responded immediately and heard her little voice. "Hello, it's me." For once she didn't address me as 'Dr. Gilbert'. I pushed the buzzer and was at the door when she arrived.

She was wearing a multicolored, silky dress and high heels. She did not look at all like the little undergraduate student that she was. I thought of her as the most sexy sample of femininity that I had ever seen.

She turned and kicked off her heels. In a quick look I noticed a particular racial characteristic — the somewhat protruding 'derrière'. I was reminded of a movie I had seen of the dancers at the Carnival in Rio.

She came back toward me and flung herself into my arms. Her filmy dress was not sufficient to insulate me from the warmth of her body. She stepped back as I guided her toward the bedroom. From then on, she took over. She pushed me onto the bed and began undressing me.

When I was on my back, completely nude, she started with a deep kiss. Her tongue ran back and forth along my lips and into my mouth. She came down along my body extended her kiss to my intense erection. Those thick lips touched me and slid down until my penis was almost entirely in her mouth. With very slow movement and gently increasing pressure she brought me to a climax like I had never known. She continued licking up my juice as if it were icing on a cake. "Oh, but you taste so good," she cried!

I thought of a line from my student days, but I couldn't remember who said it: "To fuck is human; to be blown, divine."

I was completely relaxed, as she held me. Little-by-little I started caressing her. Now it was my turn. She helped me a bit to undue the little items under that silky dress. When I had finished undressing her I took a long look at her body. It was a beautiful form, sculpted from a piece of milk chocolate. She had full, round breasts. One nipple rose between my fingers — as did the other when I took it in my mouth. Strange, she didn't taste like chocolate. I felt that my battery was being recharged, as I went down on her.

As I continued to lick her tickly mound, she reached down and opened the entrance to her secret garden. She began to moan with increasing intensity as my tongue touched her clitoris. She screamed out with her orgasm as I quickly went up and entered her — and continued until I came with her.

We lay in each others arms for a some time, how long I had no idea. When she whispered, "I have to leave now, as my parents will be expecting me at home. I'll see you tomorrow at the lab." We got up and dressed quickly. I accompanied her to the door, where she stopped to give me another deep kiss.

The scenario was repeated often. However, when we saw each other at the University, we tried to have no more than the usual exchange between student and teacher. Although, it was true that she came to my office much more often than other students.

THE EVENTS

BACK IN THE LAB, THAD was bent over his new optical system. I had just received a grant for its purchase, several thousand dollars. Thad's job was to align the mirrors — a very difficult task, as the infrared light is not visible to the human eye. He heard a little noise behind him and looked up to see Morton.

Morton James, or 'Mort' as he was often called, was a little, somewhat strange individual. He was, at least in principle, working on an advanced degree in chemistry. He was everywhere in the chemistry building, although what he was doing was not always obvious.

The infrared mirrors were indeed beautiful. They were of course first-surface mirrors, those with the reflective coating in front, rather than behind the glass, as in visual optics. The coating is therefore very fragile and should of course never be touched.

Thad finished the alignment of the mirrors and went off to lunch. When he returned he found that the optical system was no longer correctly adjusted. Several mirrors had been turned. He couldn't imagine what had happened. Then, through the afternoon he re-adjusted the system. However, the next morning he found once again that everything had been changed. The mirrors had been displaced.

Mort came in to look over his shoulder and Thad became worried about the presence of 'Mort the wart', as he had become known in the Department.

After lunch when Thad returned to the lab, he was shocked to find the optical system of his spectrometer completely ruined. Someone had broken all the mirrors. He came running up to my office. He was in tears. "The spectrometer has been smashed. All of our work is completely destroyed." I went downstairs with him to inspect what was left of our investment — in both time and money.

What Thad had said was true. "But, why would anyone do that," I asked? "I just don't know," he replied. "However, almost everyone in the Department has access to this lab. And, I do have a suspicion, as Mort has been here watching me almost every day. However, I don't see why he would do such a thing." I replied, "Yes, Thad, I agree, but we certainly can't accuse Mort, or anyone else, without some proof. I'll look into the question immediately and will also see what I can do to have the optical system replaced. I doubt if it can be repaired."

I went back up to my office and called the Police. Two plain-clothes men came very rapidly to inspect the damage to the instrument. After a quick look, one of them said, "Don't touch anything, I'll call the expert, as there are some beautiful fingerprints on those mirrors."

A half-an-hour later, a young man arrived with his attaché case. He dusted the broken mirrors and some other elements of the instrument. He then remarked, "There is only one set of prints on the mirrors, but of course I'll need to have others for comparison. These results will be on record and the Chief will be contacting you soon."

I went up to see Mr. Watson to explain what had happened. "Well," he said, "You probably should have checked with the Dean before you called in the Police, but I understand that it was urgent. In general, the University likes to avoid bad publicity, if you understand what I mean." "Yes, of course," I replied. "I'm sorry if I have caused a problem, but it would be good to have some evidence. What we need now is some finger prints of a suspect. Without making any accusation, I would like to have some good finger prints of the little wart. You remember the acid-painting incident last year."

He replied, "Yes sure, I have an idea. Tomorrow Donald Dines has his final oral exam, so there will be the usual little party afterwards. This morning his friend, Rick, asked me for one of the big fish tanks that we use for constant-temperature baths, so I assume that he is making the traditional punch. I'll offer to provide the paper cups. I will put an 'X' on the bottom of one of them and make sure that it is given to Morton." "That's a clever idea," I remarked. "And for a second time, should I address you as 'Mr. Holmes'?" "Oh, not really," he laughed, "I'm just Mr. Watson — and I'm not even a doctor."

That afternoon I got a phone call from the Dean. He expressed his regret for the damage to the 'scientific instrument' and assured me that the University would cover the cost of its replacement. He said that it would be sufficient for me to send him a copy of the company's estimate. He insisted that it was not necessary, or even advisable, for me to make further contact with the Police.

The next morning in the Department the preparations for the little party began. Rick appeared with a tall, unusually attractive young lady whom he introduced as his wife, Rita. They started preparing the room for the after-exam ceremony. They had brought in a big paper table cloth and the necessary elements for the punch. Legally, no alcohol could be included, but it always was. Mr. Watson came in with the fish tank, all scrubbed out for the occasion and a couple of big packages of paper cups. While we were decorating the table with the usual chips and things, I thought, "How did a little, rather insignificant guy like Rick manage to hook such a beautiful lady?"

The exam, the thesis oral, was not yet over but the grad students started to appear. However, Mr. Watson insisted that they couldn't start on the punch until Donald, the new Dr. Dines, came in. When he finally did, the room was getting a bit crowded. Mr. Watson had laid out the cups on a big tray and was filling them with punch. I noticed that he went directly to Morton and offered him a cup from the corner of the tray.

I saw Margo at the side of the room. She gave me a charming smile, but kept her distance. It was certainly better to keep our relationship discrete, although I knew that some of my colleagues already suspected it.

There were, of course, all the 'congratulations' to the new Dr., who had just accepted a 'post doc' at a nearby university. When the crowd began to thin out, I overheard Rita say to her husband, "I have some errands to run, so I'll see you at home." A few minutes later Jim came over to me to say that he was going back down to his lab. I noticed that he was carrying a full cup of punch that Rick had ladled out for him.

After the little party, I stayed to help Mr. Watson clean up. He picked up the paper cups with care and put all of them into a big bag. He said, "Oh, I'll dispose of all this stuff, and the table cloth. I carried the fish tank back to the prep room, where an assistant would wash it the next morning.

I closed my office and left the building to go home for some lunch. I had a big stack of exam papers awaiting me for the afternoon.

I didn't get far into the corrections when the telephone rang. "Hello, Dr. Gilbert, this is Mr. Watson at the Department." "Yes, hello," I responded: "What's up?" He answered with, "We have a serious problem here. We found both Jim Watkins and Rick's Missus — dead, apparently from poisoning. We have police all over the place here and it's evident that we need your testimony as to what happened at the little party after the thesis oral." "Yes, how terrible," I answered. "Naturally I'll be there immediately."

It was only a ten-minute ride on the street car down to the University — much faster than calling a taxi. I was very upset by the news of the incident. I didn't know the lady in question, but considered Jim to be a close friend — the first that I had made here. Then, I thought of the little wart. He had already been identified as a psychopathic case. Could he have been responsible for such a thing?

Upon my arrival at the Chemistry Building I found it invaded by policemen in uniform, and what were apparently plain-clothes men. I identified myself as Dr. Gilbert and was immediately escorted downstairs to the infrared lab. There, in Jim's little office I saw, with horror, Jim and Rita, Rick's wife, on the floor. I said to myself, "What a beautiful couple. Oh, yes, now I can imagine their relationship."

The bodies hadn't been moved. They were about to be examined by the police medics. I was asked by Inspector Dicks to identify the bodies. I said, "I have known Jim Hawkins for several years. He was a student down in the Medical School who had been working for some months here in my research lab. As for the lady, I met her only this morning at the thesis party. Her husband introduced her as 'Rita'. The family name is, as I remember, Richardson." The Inspector responded, "Thank you, Dr. Gilbert, for you testimony."

I left the building with an overpowering feeling of sadness. I had felt close to Jim and had only this morning admired Rita. I asked myself, "How could it have happened?" I started to understand some things, but certainly not all.

The next day I got some feedback from the Police. They said that there would be a formal investigation later, but they had found that the cup from which both victims had drunk contained a significant amount of cyanide, although the fish tank showed no trace. They also indicated that three sets of fingerprints were found on the cup: those of the two victims — plus, those of Morton James.

Later that morning I met with Dr. Fillmore in his office. We went over the background of the event, various persons in the Department and, in particular, the strange little wart. Dr. Fillmore indicated that we should arrange to see the Dean.

He picked up the phone and dialed. "Hello, Dean Martinson? This is Dr. Fillmore in Chemistry; I'm here with Dr. Gilbert. If you have a few minutes, I think it would be good to discuss yesterday's tragedy. Yes? We could come now." And aside he asked me, "Is that OK?" I replied with a nod and Dr. Fillmore continued with, "We'll be right up."

We walked up the hill to the old Administration building; it must have been one of the first to be built on the campus. We entered the Office of the Dean, where we were greeted by an obviously efficient administrative secretary. She led us directly into the inner sanctum and found Dean Martinson sitting behind a huge mahogany desk in the middle of a heavily furnished office. He stood up to greet us with hand shakes and a welcoming smile. He was tall and fair-skinned; I would have described him as 'a handsome Italian'. (Some ladies would ask, 'Aren't they all?') I wouldn't have considered him to be 'colored', but when we shook hands, he raised his left hand and I noticed the faint line along the side opposite the thumb. It's one of the little traces of the Negroid race that remains, even after several generations as 'high yellows'.

The Dean invited us to sit down and we immediately entered into the discussion of the duel murder in the Chemistry Department. Clearly, the University Administration was aware of the events and, in particular, the apparent role of Morton James. In spite of all efforts to hush up the story, it had reached the papers, where it was assumed to be obvious that the little wart was guilty. Furthermore, the Dean mentioned that he had just received a call from the Police. They had checked back in their files and found that the fingerprints that they had taken earlier from the smashed optical instrument matched those of Morton James.

In the course of the discussion, I remarked, "Please let me add that I think, and sincerely hope, that I have been integrated into this community. An event such as we have witnessed here can take place, and does indeed happen, in any and all societies. I hope that the publicity does not have a dueterious effect on the image of the University — and our department."

The Dean thanked me profusely for my reflections and, as we were about to leave his office, Dr. Fillmore added, "Dean Martinson, I should like to point out that Dr. Gilbert has directed the thesis work of three of our graduate students in Chemistry. They are in the first group to obtain the Ph.D. in our University. Furthermore, Dr. Gilbert has obtained important financial support from the exterior. It has not only provided the students with suitable stipends, but has made a substantial contribution to the research budget of our department."

The Dean responded with, "I'm very pleased to learn a bit more about Dr. Gilbert's accomplishments. I was already aware of some of them, and his important contributions to research and teaching in our university."

We went out of the Administration Building and walked on down the hill. I had the impression that we had had a favorable contact with the Dean, in spite of the recent event that was still our preoccupation.

THE SEQUEL

A FEW WEEKS LATER I RECEIVED a call from the Dean. He greeted me with, "Hello, Doctor. Gilbert? This is Dean Martinson. Would you have a few minutes free this morning? I would like to chat." I responded, "But, of course, Dean Martinson. I can come right away if you wish." "Yes, that would be fine," he said. "I'll expect you then in a few minutes."

I hiked back up the hill to the Administration Building and entered the Dean's office. The secretary was there, as usual. She announced that he was expecting me, I assumed that the subject was the passed events in the Chemistry Department, although they had been somewhat calmed with the arrest of 'Wart' and the passage of time. However, they were of course too important to have been forgotten.

The Dean greeted me with a handshake and invited me to sit down before his huge desk. He then addressed me, "Doctor Gilbert, I asked you to come up because I have heard some rumors that are perhaps not true. They concern your relations with a certain young co-ed here. Without asking questions, I should like simply to make a suggestion — and a proposition."

I was not completely surprised by his introduction, as he went on to say, "I know that you have very good scientific connections abroad and I think that it would be a good time for you to take advantage of them. I have learned from Dr. Fillmore that you have been invited to read a paper at an important colloquium in Paris. Let me make a proposition. If you would be in agreement to take a leave-of-absence for a few months, I can arrange for the University to pay your travel expenses. Dr. Fillmore has also indicated that you have an excellent research budget from a science foundation and can thus cover your own salary for the period. I should like to have your thinking on this proposal."

I responded without hesitation that I would be quite pleased to accept his suggestion and thanked him for his offer for the travel funds. He didn't have to remind me that if he had proof of my relations with Margo, the University would have grounds for my dismissal. It was evident that we were both thinking the same thing.

We stood up at the same instant and shook hands. He said, "Good luck and 'bon voyage'. We hope that you will be back at your post here in the near future." I was sure that he felt, as I did, that it was unlikely.

I left the Administration building and walked back down the hill. And so, now what? I really wanted to go to France, at least for the meeting in Paris. But, as to the future, I was quite uncertain. I had my research group here and a good budget to continue it. However, did I really want to stay here? Perhaps, as it represented security. Was that a primary question at this period in my life? Maybe — but I wasn't convinced.

I passed between the Doric columns into the Chemistry building. On down the hall I went into the Faculty Room, where there was the array of pigeon holes. The morning mail had been distributed. Among a handful of junk I found one of those almost-square, airmail envelopes from France. I saw that it was from Mlle. Josik at the Sorbonne. I opened it with impatience and read.

Mon Cher Ami,

I was very pleased to have talked with you on several occasions at the recent Gordon Conference. As I indicated, we would be very happy to have you here as a guest. I know that in America one often has the Summer months free of teaching duties and thus you might be able to come to Paris. I am certain that we could pay you for, say, the three Summer months. In exchange, we would be looking forward to two or three seminars on the subject of your research in spectroscopy. Of course we would expect you to lecture in French. But, I know that you would have little difficulty to do that for us.

With my pleasant souvenir of our chats, I am looking forward to the possibility of your visit.

Marie Josik, Professor

I was immediately excited about her invitation and most impressed by her English. I only wished that my French was as good.

But, what about Margo? Would she be willing to go with me to Paris? I then realized how important she had become in my life. Yes, I had to admit it to myself.

That afternoon I presented her the surprise: "This morning I received a letter from Paris. You know what? I've been invited to give some lectures at the University of Paris." "Oh, how marvelous, how do you pronounce it, the Sorbonne?" "Yes, that's right," I responded, "It's called the 'Sore Bun' — and don't you dare make a bad joke!" She started giggling and I saw tears in her big, beautiful eyes. "Please, please take me with you to Paris. I've always dreamed of going there."

THE SEQUEL

THE NEXT MORNING I PHONED the French Line. My mother used to refer to it is the CGT, for 'Compagnie Générale Transatlantique', but that abbreviation now represented the most important labor union in France. She had taken the 'Île de France' with me when I was a small boy. We had made the trip to visit my two aunts, who were still living in Normandie at that time.

When I called the French Line I was informed that their new ship, 'Le France', was now in regular service between New York and Le Havre. I inquired about booking a passage from New York around the end of May. I explained that I wanted a cabin for two — in cabin class. The gentleman proposed a sailing for May 30 and quoted the price for round-trip tickets. He, added that he assumed that we would be returning. I responded positively to his offer, but indicated that I'd have to discuss it with my lady. Furthermore, we wouldn't be able to specify the return date, so asked if it could be left open. He indicated that it would be OK and that he would hold the reservation for a few days to allow us to consider his proposal. He said that he would send us a package of information concerning the French Line and, in particular, 'Le France'. I gave him my name and address and thanked him for the information.

After my lecture that morning I returned to my office to find Margo waiting for me. "Hi," she said, "What news?" I answered, "You'll have to wait 'till this afternoon, as it's complicated — but all good!"

That afternoon she arrived at my place much earlier than usual. We were both even more excited on this occasion. All we could do was to talk about 'the trip'. "May 30 will be perfect as the graduation is the previous week. I'll have to tell my parents that I got a French fellowship and that I'll be going with a student group." She added that her father, in particular, would be very impressed and not ask too many questions.

I then reminded Margo that to go to France she would have to have a passport. "Oh," she said, "I hadn't thought about that. How do I get one?" I explained: "You'll have to go down to the Passport Office on K street. You will need some money, maybe ten dollars or so. And, you'll have to have a couple of photos. The passport people are very fussy about them. However, there is a shop next door where you can get a picture taken. It must be in a certain format, so you can't just use any picture you may have. The photographer knows the rules. You should go right away, to the Passport Office, as it takes a couple of weeks for the document to be delivered.

I decided that the next thing to do was to answer Mlle. Josik's letter. I spent some time trying to compose a letter in French, but with no great success. My French was like that of a young child who hadn't learned yet to read or write. Finally, I wrote in English, with apologies, to explain our program and the expected arrival date in Paris.

The days seemed long, as we awaited the end of May. However, I was occupied with the preparation of final exams and the correction of papers. Margo, too, was very busy, as she had her exams a bit earlier, followed by the big ceremony — the graduation exercises, at which she would receive her Bachelor's Degree in Chemistry.

I received a letter from Mlle. Josik by return mail. She said that she had reserved a room for us for the night of our arrival in Paris. She gave the address of a small hotel on Rue Madame and said that we could stay there until we found an apartment. She also gave me her addess at the University and her telephone number, and asked me to telephone the following day so that we could make plans for our stay in Paris.

When the day of the departure came — in fact it was the day before, as we had that long train ride to New York to take first. I had told Margo to call a cab, load her suitcases and give her driver my address. "When he gets to my place, tell him to wait with you. I'll be ready at nine with my stuff, so we can go on to Union Station. Don't forget to prepare one suitcase with the things you'll need for the trip. The others can be checked."

The taxi arrived with Margo and several suitcases. The driver loaded mine into the trunk, while Margo and I exchanged big hugs. Within fifteen minutes we were at the side of Union Station, where a baggage man was just pushing up a cart. When he and the driver had loaded the cart, it was my turn to tip the 'cabbie' for his service. It was just the beginning of what I was soon to learn: A tourist travels with a hand in his pocked, ready to pass out money at every turn.

We walked into the station with the baggage man pushing the cart. He turned to us and asked, "Whe's y'all goin'?" I was proud of my understanding of the local accent when I explained that we were going to New York to take a ship to France. He responded with, "Bon voyage, Monsieur et Dame". I handed him a handsome tip with a handshake. He was yet another 'integrated' Haitian in Washington.

Inside the Station we bought two tickets to New York and checked the baggage through to the French Line pier. Our train was waiting for us, as we walked down the platform hand-in-hand — for the first time in public — and said goodbye to Washington.

The train pulled out from Union Station and we were on our way into the unknown. We were both happy, but I was sure that Margo shared my feeling of concern for what the future might bring.

It was long. I reviewed my trip down to Washington — like playing a home movie backwards. Stops at Baltimore, Wilmington, Philadelphia, Trenton and finally, Newark — where we didn't get off. I remembered it so well: The Research Center of course, but did my old Ford get sold? Such un-important thoughts.

I squeezed Margo's hand as we saw the skyline of New York in the distance. Then, it all disappeared as we went under the Hudson river for the arrival at Penn station.

Margo said that she had come 'up here' a couple of times with her parents and her younger brother. However, they had driven. They had not visited New York, but had preferred to continue into New England. She explained that once they were north of Boston, they felt relieved of racial problems. They could go into a restaurant without fear of being mistreated. I had to admit that I had never thought about that problem.

"We'll see New York next time", I promised. "Just now we have the big boat to take tomorrow morning." I explained that we had a room reserved at the Baldwin, a little hotel down in Greenwich Village, not too far from the French Line pier.

We went up to the huge hall of Penn Station and out to the street, where we took a taxi. We checked into the hotel and left our things in the room. We were both tired from the long train trip, but happy to walk a bit in the 'Village'. We had dinner at a little Italian restaurant, then continued our walk before returning to the hotel to collapse for the night. We were both too tired to profit from our first night together.

Early the next morning we packed our suitcases, grabbed a bite of breakfast and took a taxi for the short ride to the French Line pier. There, we presented our tickets and deposited our stuff. We were told that all of it, our cabin baggage, would be put directly aboard ship. It would go through French Customs in the boat-train from Le Havre to Paris. The rest of our luggage, that had been checked through from Washington, would be waiting for us in Paris at the Gare St. Lazarre, where it would go through Customs. All was very well-organized.

As we were now free of our luggage, I suggested that we walk back to look at the ship. It was very impressive — three times the length of a football field! Back under the elevated West Side Highway we saw one of the local inhabitants. He was sitting on a pile of newspapers, with an old, very dirty blanket and a nearly empty bottle next to him. He gave Margo a long look and made the comment — more-or-less to himself: "What a dirty shame, what a goddam dirty shame". And spit in our general direction. We walked back to the ship, our last few steps in America.

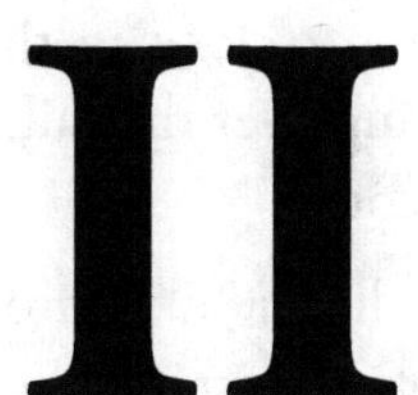

OFF TO PARIS!

WE PRESENTED OUR TICKETS AND passed immediately up the gangplank. We were welcomed there by a steward, who led us immediately to our stateroom. It was modern, in good taste, and of course impeccable. We found all of our hand baggage and took a few minutes to 'freshen up', as the English like to say. We then set out to explore the ship.

On board there were many festivities. Bottles of Champagne were to be seen in every corner. Many visitors were there to celebrate the departure of family and friends. Some were even decked out in evening dress, although it was only ten o'clock in the morning. We just visited the ship and spent time looking over the rail at the Statue of Liberty and other landmarks on the horizon.

Finally, there was the call for all visitors to leave the ship. They apparently did so, but it took almost another two hours. And then, the ship started very slowly to move. It was being tugged out of the harbor by several incredibly small boats. Little-by-little the New York skyline began to fade into the distance. The pilot descended to make his return in another small boat, and we were officially on our way.

Just as we lost sight of land, the announcement for lunch was made. We found our way to the Cabin Class dining room and were seated with another couple. They were also Americans, on their way to Europe for the first time. It was for six weeks or so to see the key spots — London, Paris and a bit of Italy.

The waiter presented the menu for the mid-day meal. It was no lunch. There were ten or so dishes from which to choose — but only for the first course! After that came the 'plat de résistance'. Again there was considerable choice, ranging from Long Island duck in an orange sauce ('Canard à l'orange') to a roast leg of lamb with potato cakes ('Gigot d'agneau, pommes Dauphines'). For the most part there was no linguistic problem, as most culinary terms in English are French.

We then rather expected desserts, but no, with a look at the menu we understood, as a magnificent green salad with 'vinaigrette' followed. And then the waiter arrived with a sort of cart — a table on wheels on which was displayed at least twenty kinds of cheese. Each was identified by its region of origin (in France, of course). After a pause, as we tried to imagine the followup, there appeared another cart with desserts — all kinds of pastries with creams and fruits that were completely beyond our imaginations and beginning to surpass our capacities. It goes without saying that each course (except the salad) was accompanied with an appropriate wine. Here again, with the arrival of the wine waiter (the 'sommelier') the origin and the vintage was announced. We were snowed, as the students would say, by the whole presentation.

After the meal we went out on deck to look at the endless sea. We found chaises-longues and settled down for the afternoon. But we had hardly had a chance to snooze when a waiter came by with the afternoon tea and an array of scones. And that evening back in the dining room, the menu was equally elaborate.

After dinner I asked Margo for her first impressions. "Oh it's great, but the meals are terribly complicated", she replied. "However, I find that the dishes are quite tasteless — not at all what I'm used to." I laughed and remarked, "Yes, I know that it's not like hog maws and chitterlings, strongly dosed with hot peppers, but it's what you'll find in classic French cooking."

Every day the clocks were turned ahead an hour. Each passenger adjusted his watch so that on arrival in Europe he would be on time and wouldn't notice the six hours 'lost' along the way.

Each evening there was a floorshow, complete with a band, a singer, and many people in evening dress. At one point people started to dance. Almost immediately, a tall, handsome fellow came to our table and asked, first my permission, and then Margo, if she would like to dance. After my OK, they took a swing around the dance floor. I had to admit that I enjoyed watching Margo dance, particularly when it turned to a South

American tune. She obviously had what was referred to as 'that natural rhyme'. It was a pleasant contrast to the stiff French ladies who wore a rather smug look — never a trace of a smile.

Margo was breathless as she was ushered back to the table, where the gent in question thanked me with a bow. He was clearly impressed by Margo, her dancing — and probably much more.

She took her place at the table and asked me, "Don't you like to dance?" "Oh, no," I answered, "Several young ladies have tried to teach me, but it's hopeless. I just can't get interested. And for the most part, I detest the music." She looked disappointed. And, in a certain sense I was too.

A couple of days later we were again on deck watching the sea. I asked Margo what she thought of the voyage. "Frankly, I find it boring", she replied. I didn't respond with what I was thinking. I just said, "I'm sorry". I realized that as we got better acquainted, it was apparent that we had quite different tastes.

It was very early in the morning when the whistle sounded. I got up to look out the porthole. It was just getting light, but was very foggy. I said, "Hurry up and get dressed! We are approaching land."

A few minutes later we went up on deck. It was cold. Through the fog we could just make out some buildings on the English coast. As we were tugged into the port of Southampton, we could see the activity on the dock. Many men were hurrying along, preparing to disembark baggage and, presumably, passengers. A bit later for the first time and the last morning on board, we ate breakfast.

Through the morning we prepared our hand baggage. Finally, at lunch the ship began to move and when we go up on deck we could see the French coast in the distance. There were numerous freighters to be seen and we were told that the Channel at this point was probably the busiest waterway in the World. There were other passenger ships, ferries and freighters, as well as many small boats for fishing and pleasure.

As we approached Le Havre, a group of small boats came out to greet us. One of them pulled up and we saw the pilot board the ship. The others were there to tug us into the harbor. From our position on the port side of the ship, we saw a long wharf with many cars moving to and fro.

The tiny vehicles looked like toys in the distance and even up close they were little by American standards.

Then, there was an announcement in several languages telling passengers to prepare their hand luggage. It went on to explain that passengers going directly to Paris should get their reservations for their places on the boat train and have their luggage tagged by the steward who would come to our stateroom after we docked. It was all perfectly organized.

We went down the gangplank and were immediately led to our compartment in the boat train. Our baggage had already been installed in the racks above our heads. We found the train rather quaint. Each car was divided into compartments for six passengers and their suitcases. There were two other couples there, speaking English with a terribly British accent.

We pulled out of the station, and through the late afternoon, continued our trip to Paris. I remarked, "Margo, this is Normandie. Can you imagine that I was here with my mother when I was four years old? Honestly, I don't remember it." "No, of course not," she replied, "I can't imagine it, but for me it all looks the same here — although on a smaller scale than we know in the U.S." Clearly, Margo was not impressed.

At a certain moment two uniformed agents came to our compartment. They checked our passports and took a summary look at our suitcases in the rack above. They said that for what we had checked through, we could pass customs anytime within the next three days at Gare St. Lazarre.

In the evening we pulled into the Gare. Some passengers lowered the windows and started throwing their suitcases out onto the platform. We looked on with amazement, took down our own baggage and lugged it out the door. Clearly, we were not familiar with the customary procedures. Fortunately, we had very little hand baggage, as we headed out through the station to the taxi stand.

THE ARRIVAL

Night had fallen as the taxi driver stowed our hand baggage and we got into the tiny vehicle. I give the driver the address of the hotel on Rue Madame, where Mlle. Josik had reserved a room for us. We darted out into a maze of little, dark streets. What seemed strange, absolutely bizarre, none of the cars had their headlights on. A driver would flash them on just as he approached an unsuspecting pedestrian. We just held our collective breath.

We had no idea where we were, although we passed a huge, very brightly lighted square. Then, we crossed a river — the Seine, of course. We continued at the same frantic speed along a boulevard and then through another series of dark streets, before jerking to a stop. The driver announced, "Voilà, nous sommes arrivés". I paid the fare and added the 15%, as I had been warned to do.

At the little reception desk I identified myself as 'Jacques Gilbert'. The lady handed me a couple of keys and indicated the stairway with a gesture. As we climbed up the stairs, I understood why our suitcases were called 'luggage'. On the second floor (Which was referred to there as the first) we found number 17, as marked on the key tags.

The hotel room was small and neat, equipped with the essential — a bed. Besides the usual washbowl there was a low piece of plumbing that Margo noticed. She immediately inquired, "What's that thing?" I explained, "Oh yes, in the travel books that I studied before we left, it was mentioned. It was referred to as a 'douche bowl', used for feminine hygiene. However, according to my mother it serves also to wash private parts of either sex, as well as to wring out socks and underwear."

There was an adjoining little room that was equipped with a toilet and, separated by a sort of screen, a strange looking bathtub. The tub was square with a sort of ledge inside that apparently was to sit on. Although the tub was not suitable for reclining, it could be used for a wash-up. So much for the minor differences between countries. When we organized our things, we found that all was the same in bed, as we knew back in 'America'. We didn't even remember that we had skipped the evening meal.

The next morning I picked up the telephone and in my hesitant French ordered breakfast for two. Margo exclaimed, "You mean they bring us breakfast in bed? That's great!" And so they did, as ten minutes later there was a tap at the door and a lady arrived with a tray. It was loaded with a hunk of 'baguette', butter, jam and croissants, as well as little pitchers of hot, very strong coffee and milk. The maid discretely presented the tray on the table next to the bed, without a glance in the direction of the couple in it.

After breakfast, as Margo was getting dressed, etc., I picked up the Michelin guide and studied the area. We were in the sixth arrondissement, as the districts in French cities are described, close to the Luxembourg gardens. I planned our morning walk to the Latin Quarter and Notre Dame. I then understood our taxi ride of the night before. When we saw the bright lights we were passing the Champs Elysées at the 'Place de la Concorde'. Then we crossed the Seine, before taking a long boulevard (Raspail) and plunging again into darkness before arriving at the hotel.

When Margo was ready we went downstairs, left the keys at the reception desk and stepped out on to the street — Rue Madame. We turned down a side street and arrived at an entrance to the Jardin de Luxembourg. We entered through an open gate and went down a gravel path under the trees. At one side there was a tennis court, where two enthusiastic young men were engaged in a match. They were dressed in the traditional tennis outfits, white shorts and T-shirts. The court was in clay, that is 'terre battue', but I noticed that the color was quite different from what I knew in Washington. Here, it was reddish, rather than grey, indicating an important concentration of iron oxide. The player's shoes were red with dust.

We came out from under the trees and saw the Palais de Luxembourg on our left. In front of us was a very big basin, where a number of children were sailing their little boats. Several baby carriages were nearby, each with a maid or 'nurse' in a white apron sitting on a bench. I noticed a somewhat hunched lady in a blue smock who was collecting money from each person seated on a bench. I remarked to Margo, "Can you imagine that one has to pay to sit on a bench?"

Further on there were many flower gardens. Each one was very formally laid out in true French style. All were colorful and, of course, impeccable. We then passed back under the trees and along another gravel path. It led to a gate, opening onto a 'place' at the intersection of several streets with Boulevard Saint Michel. Up ahead we could see the Panthéon. I told Margo that this monument (according to what I had read that morning) is dedicated to famous people in French history.

We tuned down Boulevard Saint Michel and a couple of blocks later arrived in front of the Sorbonne. "Here it is!" I exclaimed, "Maybe I'll be giving my lectures here — I don't know. By the way, we'll have to see Mlle. Josik, the Professor here, to schedule my talks. Maybe we should go this afternoon. I'll try to phone her later."

We continued our walk through the Latin Quarter. We passed the Cluny museum and continued several more blocks. Along the way were many students and tourists, like us. I noticed that, as in Washington, the Asian and African ladies were in their traditional dress, while the men wore European clothes. There were several newsstands, with newspapers and magazines in various languages. The kiosks, round cylinders covered with posters of all kinds were, we thought, very strange — picturesque.

At the foot of Boul' Mich', as the students called it, we arrived at the Seine. Across was the Île de la Cité, mostly covered with administrative buildings. But at right, there she was, Notre Dame de Paris, most certainly the best-known cathedral in the World. We crossed to the square in front of the Cathedral. It was swarming with tourists from all comers of the World. We entered and were welcomed by the cool air and the calm atmosphere. Neither of us was Catholic, but we understood the significance of this very special place.

"I wish I knew more about architecture", I remarked, "How did they design, let alone build, such a structure? It gives the impression of reaching up to the sky. And look at the light through the rose window! We'll have to study and come back with a better understanding." "Sure, OK", Margo replied. She was certainly impressed, but less interested in the history and architecture than I was. We both realized that it was time for some lunch, so we went out and headed up a little street. Margo notice the sign, 'Rue de la Harpe'. "That's a cute name", she commented.

We went into a tiny restaurant, obviously a 'papa-and-mama' establishment. We were seated with several others, mostly students, at a long table covered with a paper tablecloth. There were several bottles of wine along the middle of the table, as well as baskets filled with hunks of bread. The slate board on the wall announced the dishes for the day, if one could read the handwriting. The fixed-price menu included an hors-d'œuvre, the 'plat de jour' and cheese or dessert. We were astounded by the price, 300 francs – less than one dollar! We did notice that 15%, the required tip, was added to the bill. It was still a bargain and excellent.

After lunch we continued up Rue de la Harpe that rejoined St. Michel and continued to Rue de Vaugirard. We took the walk along it (The guide Michelin mentioned that it was the longest street in Paris) to our street, Rue Madame. Back at our hotel I asked the lady at the desk if she could telephone for me, as I was unaccustomed to the telephone system. I gave here the number that Mlle. Josik had sent me, and when, after some "allo, allo, allo…", reached a soprano voice. I asked for, "Mademoiselle le Professeur Josik". She answered with, "Oui, Monsieur, ne quittez pas". When Mlle. Josik responded, I introduced myself and she immediately replied in English. She asked about our trip and then suggested that we come to her office the following morning. I said that we had her address and could probably find the way.

The next morning we took one of those green and yellow buses to the Jardin des Plantes. The bus was, to us at least, very quaint. When it stopped we got on the back — on a sort of platform, where stood a uniformed man. We then proceeded down the central aisle until we found two places free. We heard a bell, 'ding-ding', and I looked around to see that the man on the platform had pulled a cord that hung from above. The bus started and the uniformed 'contôleur' came up the aisle and stood beside us. He asked our destination and when I replied, he turned a crank on a big box that was strapped to his round 'tummy'. A ticket was printed for each of us with the price printed on it. I paid him the amount indicated. He thanked us, and returned to his place on the rear platform. At the following stops this routine was repeated for each arriving passenger.

We got off at the entrance to the garden and entered through the open gate. It was a very impressive scene. In the center was a series of formal gardens, separated by paths. On the right side were large trees and far in the distance what appeared to be a big green house. On the left were several buildings, which, as we learned later, were museums — paleontology, mineralogy, etc. "All of this to be visited leisurely", I thought.

Turning right through the trees, we found the animals. It was a small zoo with a number of species of birds and mammals. Behind the zoo, passing through a small exit gate, we arrived at Rue Cuvier. Further down, on the other side of the street at the address that Mlle. Josik had given me was an old building — part of the University of Paris. We entered and went up a flight of stairs. Along the hallway, near the end, was a door marked 'MLLE. LE PROFESSEUR JOSIK'. At our knock we heard, "Entrez". Her secretary was sitting behind a desk in a corner. She was probably in her late twenties, with a pleasant smile, and rather ordinary 'looks'. Before I could finish our introduction, Mlle. Josik hurried out of her office to shake hands.

MADEMOISELLE LE PROFESSEUR

I INTRODUCED MARGO TO MLLE. JOSIK and explained that she had studied French in college, but was not yet fluent. Mlle. Josik introduced her secretary as Janine, then addressed Margo in English. "By the end of the summer you'll have solved the problem." She then invited us into her office, small and quite simply furnished, and offered us chairs. She asked us about the trip and our first impressions of Paris.

The first questions were my seminars and the big meeting the first week of September. Mlle. Josik explained that the seminars were held on Thursday afternoons. She suggested that I present two during June and that we could discuss the subjects later. That would mean that your first would be Thursday of next week. Would that be alright?" "Yes, of course", I answered. She added that the program for the meeting had now been fixed and that I had been allotted twenty minutes to present the recent work of my group in Washington.

Mlle. Josik turned to Margo and suggested: "I think it would be good for you to study French while you are here. I'm sure that you two will be busy as tourists, but Jack will sometimes be preoccupied with science." "Yes, …Ma'm", Margo replied, "That's a good idea." Mlle. Josik laughed and said, "My dear girl, please call me 'Marie', as all my other friends do. Monday morning Janine can take you to the Alliance Française. They have classes in conversation all summer. By the way, your name goes very well in French, although everybody here will write it with a "t" at the end.

Then to me she remarked, "I'll call you 'Jack' rather than 'John', because it's like 'Jacques' in French — at least almost. Monday we can discuss your seminar topics, OK?" She hesitated, and then asked, "Where are you staying?" I replied that for the moment we were in the hotel room that she had reserved, but we couldn't afford to stay there all summer." "Of course not," she responded, "But I have an idea. There is a Canadian graduate student in our group who will be going back home for the summer. Perhaps you can arrange to take his little place. I'll talk to him and let you know. I know he doesn't pay too much for it."

We both thanked Marie for her help, exchanged the traditional handshakes, and agreed to meet Monday morning at nine o'clock.

As Margo and I walked down Rue Cuvier toward the Seine, we compared our impressions of the lady. She was, we agreed, a very impressive person. We took a bus back to the neighborhood of our hotel and found a small restaurant. It was like the one where we had eaten the day before, a papa-and-mama establishment, but this time there was a bar near the entrance. The barman was very probably their son.

On Monday morning we found our way back to Marie's office. Janine, the secretary, was ready to take Margo to the Alliance. I suggested to Margo that we meet at the entrance to the 'greenhouse' in the Jardin des Plantes. "OK", she said as the two young ladies hurried off.

The door to Marie's office was open, but I heard her talking on the telephone, so waited for her to finish. A few minutes later she called, "Jacques, please come in and have a seat".

"So, what are you planning to tell us about in your two seminars?" "Well", I replied, "I had thought of first, a general review, and secondly, an advanced look at recent developments — including the materiel in the communication for the meeting." "That sounds fine. Please give me tentative titles so the seminars can be announced today.

I wrote down the two titles and handed them to Marie, with the request: "Please correct my French." She read them and made a couple of suggestions, which I accepted without question.

She changed the subject with, "Now, tell me a bit about your situation." (Apparently she had guessed that I was on uncertain ground as to my future). I decided to tell her of my concern, but first asked, "My I say something rather personal?" She laughed at that. "But of course, please understand that, although I am now a lady of a certain age, I have 'been around', as they say in your country."

She gave me confidence; so I went on to explain my affaire with

Margo and the question of my tenure at the University. She asked me directly if our personal relation was good. I replied that it was, at least on the physical side. However, I remarked that we did not seem to have the same intellectual tastes.

Marie addressed me as, "My dear boy" — followed by her reflections: "You are young; enjoy it, but remember that relationships often change. You may find some day that sex is not necessarily the most important thing in life. Young couples often drift apart with time if there is nothing else to solidify their love." I asked myself, "How could she be so open, so frank? And yes, she was a most intelligent lady."

She continued, "So much for my 'mother role', although I've never been one. Now tell me what you want to do with your academic life." I gave her my honest answer: "I don't know. I have made a serious investment in time and energy to develop my research. I'm sure that I could go back to the University if I chose to. However, as you have guessed, I'm not sure that I want to."

"Yes, I understand", she nodded. "Let me think about it. For the moment you are no doubt preparing you little speech for Thursday afternoon. Have courage; it will go well. Our seminars are held in a lecture hall in our research laboratory near the Orly airport. I'll take you there. I propose that we meet here at two thirty." I thought, "Too bad, I won't get to give a lecture at the Sorbonne — maybe next time."

Marie continued, "By the way, I asked the Canadian about his little apartment. He said he would be overjoyed if you could stay there for the three months that he'll be gone — especially if you could pay his rent for the period. He will be attending your seminar, so you can get acquainted then.

I said goodbye with many thanks for her help and, in particular, her advice. I noticed that our handshake lasted an instant longer than usual, a sign of our rather intimate exchange.

I went downstairs and across the street to the little zoo. After exchanging remarks with the various animals, I wandered up through the gardens to the entrance to the 'greenhouse'. Before long I saw Margo coming along a gravel path. When I asked how it went, she exclaimed, "We took the Métro! It was great!" "OK, but how did the French go?"

I asked. "Oh, they gave me a little exam and said that I obviously had studied French and that I could enter a class in conversation. I'll be going back Monday morning to get started."

"That's very good, you shouldn't have any trouble. It's primarily a matter of self-confidence. Now, let's go into the greenhouse. It should be interesting; it's a tropical garden."

We entered and were greeted by the chattering of parrots and various other birds. The palm trees were of many different varieties, judging from their foliage. The background was in thickets of huge bamboos and other trees that I couldn't identify. We located some of the origins of the chatter. Two of them were beautiful multicolored parrots; a number of others were African greys — with their bright red tail feathers. One of the greys was sitting on a limb just above us. He looked straight at me, cocked his head, and said, "Bonjour, Jacot. Ça va?". Margo cried out in astonishment and started laughing. Just then a uniformed attendant came walking down the path. He explained, in French of course, that everybody working there greets the parrot each morning. "But we were astonished. How did he know that my name is Jacques? And, above all, when I was little my mother called me 'Jacot'." We were all amused, including Jacot.

Further along the path we reached a waterfall, with a rapids below. The atmosphere was dense, humid, heavy with the odors of the tropical flora. Margo was thrilled and later talked often of what a jungle must be like.

We left the Jardin des Plantes between two of the museum buildings and walked along Rue Buffon. On the other side of the street we found yet another small restaurant. Our lunch there was like in all the others, good, filling and cheap.

On Monday I realized that my first seminar was approaching so I stayed in the hotel room, while Margo went off for her French class. I dug out my notes from an advanced course that I had given in Washington. I jotted down bits of French vocabulary in the margins, with the aid of the little dictionary that we had brought with us. However, a number of words were too technical for it.

That afternoon I reminded Margo that we still had baggage at Gare

St. Lazarre. "Oh, that's right she said. I guess we'll have to go there."
I asked downstairs at the desk how to get to the Gare St. Lazarre. The
lady gave me the number of the bus on Boulevard Raspail that would
take us directly. At the Gare we found a window marked 'Service des
Douanes'. The lady behind the 'guichet' heard us speaking English as
we approached and asked in English, "May I help you?" She had a very
British accent. I explained that we had baggage there and presented the
check. She handed it to an employee, who disappeared in the darkness
behind her.

A few minutes later the man turned up through door on the side,
pushing a cart with our two big suitcases. He asked me to open them, and
when I did, he felt along each corner and said, "OK, you can close them.
He stamped the baggage tag to indicate that we had passed customs.
Margo turned to me and asked, "What are we going to do now. We don't
need all that stuff in our hotel room. The English lady (We learned that
she indeed was) came to our rescue and explained that we could now
leave the suitcases in check until we found lodging. Then, she said, we
could just phone and they would be delivered. She handed us a card with
the phone number and said, "Good luck. There is an enormous housing
problem in Paris." We thanked her again and went back to the hotel with
one job done.

When Thursday came Margo went to her French class as usual, while
I took a last look at my notes. When she returned we went out to one of
our little family restaurants. Afterwards I said that I would have to meet
Marie, who would take me to the CNRS lab for my seminar. I explained
that it was the abbreviation for 'Centre National de la Recherche
Scientifique'. She said that she would prefer to explore the neighborhood
a bit and wished me good luck with my speech.

I arrived at Marie's office at two thirty on the dot. She was already
there, working at her desk. She got up and led me down to a parking area
behind the building. There, she stopped before a tiny grey vehicle, like
many I had seen in the streets of Paris. "Here it is," she said, "My 'deux
chevaux'; isn't it cute?" I may have looked a bit hesitant, as she continued;
"Don't be afraid, it runs very well."

We got in, somehow. When she started the motor the sound was similar to that of a motorcycle. We bounced out of the parking lot like a small boat in a rough sea. When we arrived at a big intersection (It was Place d'Italie), I closed my eyes as we darted full speed into the maze of traffic. "Don't worry, you'll get used to it. But when you drive here, just be sure to yield to anyone on your right."

In less than fifteen minutes we arrived at a gate. A sign indicated 'Laboratoires de Recherches du CNRS'. A uniformed attendant opened the gate at the sight of our little car and gave a little salute. We parked in a spot marked 'Mlle. Josik' and entered a building. "This," she said, "Is my other home."

She led me into a lecture hall. It was fairly large, for perhaps 150 people. At the back I saw a slide projector. I asked Marie if we could run through the slides to be sure that they were in order and properly oriented. She replied, "Of course, let me get the projectionist." She went out in the hall and I heard her call him, Antoine, who came running to help us. Fortunately, I had thought to prepare the little square slides that were used everywhere in the World except the U.S. There, we always had the big, rectangular glass ones.

Assured that the slides were OK, Marie remarked that we had a bit of time to look at the lab. "In fact," she said, "I think that Gaëtan, the Canadian, is here. Let's see." We walked down the hall and entered one of the research labs. The first thing I saw was an infrared spectrometer, the same model that we had in Washington. Gaëtan was sitting at a desk in the far corner. He came immediately to greet us and was introduced.

With my first two sentences of French, he asked if I were 'Québecois'. He insisted that I had the same accent. I explained that I was from New England — from a French-speaking community. I really didn't realize that we had essentially the same accent. And it is true that one cannot recognize his own.

Gaëtan immediately asked me if Mlle. Josik had mentioned his little apartment. I replied, yes, she did, and we are very much interested. Could we come by to see it?" "Yes, certainly. Would tomorrow morning around ten be OK?" "Sure," I answered, "I'll bring my lady; where should we meet?" He suggested: "At the exit of the Métro 'Alésia'. There is a café on the corner" We agreed and shook hands. I hurried back to the lecture hall, the 'amphi', as it was called in the lab. It was over half full.

A few minutes later, Marie, that is, Mlle. Josik, introduced me as 'the young professor from America' and I received applause. In general, the talk went well, although I had a number of linguistic problems. However, when I slipped in an English word, nobody seemed to be bothered, although I was. Even some weeks later I recalled certain mistakes that I had made. They haunted me.

At the end of the lecture there were several questions. I understood perfectly, but need help to answer. However, Marie said that I had done a good job and thanked me. Just to cheer me up, she remarked that I had made very few errors in French.

As I was picking up my slides in the back of the room, a gentlemen approached and introduced himself as David Livingston He switched to English and said that he was a professor of physics in Indiana, just visiting Paris. He went on to explain that he was on leave and was acting as Dean of the 'Faculté des Sciences' in the Zaïre. He congratulated me on my lecture and remarked that my French was unusually good — for an American!

DR. LIVINGSTON

I STOOD THERE LIKE AN IDIOT, as I had no idea where the Zaïre was! He laughed and said that the 'République Démocratique du Congo', that was formally a Belgian colony, had just changed its name to 'Zaïre'. He added that it was not at all surprising that I didn't know where it was.1*

Dr. Livingston said that he would like to chat and asked if I were free for lunch tomorrow. "Of course your lady is invited too!" He remarked that Mlle. Josik had spoken of us. We agreed to meet at the Jardin des Plantes, in front of 'the green house' at midday. I figured that we should have finished our visit with Gaëtan and have time to get there.

Marie took me back into Paris in her deux chevaux and let me off at Place d'Italie. I was to take the Métro for the first time. I bought my ticket and went down through a tunnel, where I was met by a little round lady in a blue smock. She took my ticket and punched it. In future trips in the Paris Métro I had the impression that at each station it was the same little lady punching tickets. After a look at the map, I saw where to change and finally came out at 'Notre Dame des Champs'. It was only a short walk to our hotel on Rue Madame.

Margo was waiting for me, and immediately asked me how the lecture went. I replied that it was correct scientifically, but that I had problems with French — particularly in answering questions. She remarked that she didn't come because she had heard the same thing in English, and was just now a bit off of science.

"And so, what did you see here in this 'quartier'? She responded, "I found several little clothing shops nearby, on Boulevard Raspail, I think. They have some marvelous things! The styles are completely different from what we have in the U.S. and everything is handmade. Can you imagine?" I replied, 'That's nice". I had the impression the Margo had found the first thing that she really enjoyed in Paris. I noticed that she didn't buy anything, although she had some money. And, as she knew, I was willing to help out a bit if she found something she really wanted.

The next morning we took the Métro with confidence. We arrived at Alésia without error and came up at a busy intersection of several avenues and streets. The dominant feature was a church, with a 'charcuterie', a sort of specialized deli, across the street. A big sign above the entrance showed a pig, with tears running down his cheeks. And next to him was written, 'Don't cry big beast, you're going chez Noblet' (the name of the establishment). We decided that there was a difference between French humor and American. On the opposite corner we saw a café with a terrace, no doubt where we were to meet Gaëtan. It was a little too early, so we wandered around the neighborhood. We stopped in front of the cinema and studied the announcements of forthcoming movies. Margo said, "I'm afraid I won't be able to understand them." "Oh, don't worry about that, you soon will," I replied.

Near ten we walked toward the café, just as Gaëtan was arriving. He greeted us with "Salut" and took a long look at Margo. He smiled and said, "As the French like to say, 'enchanté'." He spoke perfect English, with a trace of the French-Canadian accent. I presented Margo and we followed Gaëtan down a side street. As we approached a poster advertising 'Suze', we saw that it was on a round metallic structure from which escaped the sound of running water and a terrible odor. Margo exclaimed, "Oh," and held her nose. Gaëtan laughed and explained, "That affair is very French. They call it rather vulgarly, a 'pissotière', where men go to urinate." "But what do the ladies do?" asked Margo. "It's not obvious," replied Gaëtan.

Further down the street we passed a 'boulangerie' with piles of bread, baguettes and various big loaves in the window. Nothing was wrapped, of course. At number four we followed Gaëtan in and stopped in front of a window. A lady peered out, but when she saw Gaëtan she immediately came out the door to greet us. She was perhaps in her seventies, dressed in a gray smock, and smiling as she shook hands. Gaëtan introduced her as Madame Amat. She said, "I'm pleased to meet the friends of my dear Canadian." Gaëtan explained that he would be 'going back home' for the summer and had suggested that Margo and I take his flat until his return. Turning to us he said, "Now if you want to see my little place, you'll have to work; there are three flights of stairs.

We made it, but I had to think of those two big suitcases that were still checked at Gare St. Lazarre. We found what was obviously at one time the maid's quarters that had been refurbished into a sort of studio. The big room with beams in the ceiling was very simply furnished. There was a daybed to the side and a kitchen corner that contained a two-burner gas plate, a small sink and a tiny refrigerator with a top as workspace for the 'chef'. In addition to a small table and a couple of chairs, there was one old armchair. There was an adjoining 'bathroom' with an improvised shower and a toilet. Gaëtan had constructed bookshelves out of bricks and planks of wood and, in one corner, had attached a rod to the ceiling for hanging clothes. There was only one window, through which I could see a courtyard far below. I was pleasantly surprised to note that the place was very tidy.

I looked at Margo. She seemed to be satisfied, as I remarked that we could probably get along fine here for the summer. I agreed to pay his rent and asked when the place would be free. Gaëtan laughed again, and replied, "I'll be leaving very early tomorrow morning, so all you have to do is pick up the key from Mme. Amat when you want to move in — tomorrow morning, if you want". "Yes, that would be good, as we are paying a lot for a hotel room, as well as for our checked baggage."

We said 'goodbye and bon voyage' to Gaëtan and went back to the hotel. I told the person at the desk that we would be checking out the next morning. I telephoned the English lady at Gare St. Lazarre to give her our new address and told her when we would be moving. She said that the baggage would be delivered around eleven. Good timing.

"Now," I said to Margo, "Let's celebrate; we're invited out to lunch with Dr. Livingston." "Who?" "He's an American from Indiana. I met him yesterday after my lecture. He's on leave and teaching in the Congo. Can you imagine?" "No, I can't, but let's go — where?" I replied, "Back to the tropical forest. That's appropriate, isn't it? We are to meet him at noon in front of Jacot's house."

At noon Dr. Livingston was waiting for us. I introduced Margo, "A former chemistry student of mine in Washington," I said. "Yes, I see, I'm very glad to meet you, Margo. Please call me 'Dave'." I remarked, "Although my name is Jack, our parrot friend in here (indicating the greenhouse) calls me 'Jacot'." Dave laughed and said, "You'll make many such friends in the Zaïre." He then led us out through the passage between two of the museums. We turned right on Rue Buffon and walked several blocks. On a corner, at the intersection of several diagonal streets, we saw what looked like a farmhouse. It was freshly painted white and bore a sign 'Restaurant à la Ferme'. We followed Dave in, where he was welcomed with a handshake by the headwaiter — in fact, the only waiter.

The decor of the interior was far from Parisian. On the ceiling, two large cartwheels with attached little electric bulbs served as chandeliers below the wooden beams. The walls were in white plaster, with colorful drapes at the windows. The several tables were covered with white table clothes, where the Limoges were accompanied by polished silverware. In all, it gave the impression of being immaculate, without an air of sterility.

We were shown to our table and presented with the menus. I noticed that ours did not indicate the prices, although most certainly that handed to Dave did. He was given the 'carte des vins', which he immediately passed over to me — with the comment, "I don't know anything about wine."

After we had ordered, Dave started to talk about his work in the Zaïre. He explained, for Margo's benefit, that the name had been changed. He spoke briefly of the politics after the independence from Belgium, the successive influences of the Soviets, the Japanese, and the Americans. He went on to explain," The civil war, which was a major revolt by the Simbas in the Eastern part of the country, has now been put down. It resulted in a considerable amount of destruction and much loss of life in that area. The Belgians were, for the most part, chased out after Independence, but the many other foreigners, mostly there as missionaries, suffered immensely. Stanleyville, now called Kisangani, was occupied by the revolting 'Simbas' for more than three months. Finally, the UNO sent paratroups to free the European hostiges. By the way the word 'simba' means lion in Swahili."

"Oh, yes," I remarqued, "I remember that Stanleyville was named after the explorer. And wasn't it in that area where he met a certain Mr. Livingston?" "But of course, but it is purely coincidental that with my name I should be working in the former Stanleyville!"

"And why am I in Kisangani? Well, we are trying to build a small university — more like a college in the American style. We have financial support from the 'outside', primarily from various Protestant organizations in Scandinavia, England, and the United States. Those of us who have decided to help out have come without interest in the religious question, but to help contribute to the education of the people. It is hard to imagine a country where there is no system of education — no public schools, either elementary or secondary. However, there remains the Catholic University in Kinshasa, formerly Leopoldville, that is now a Government institution, as well as a smaller establishment at Lubumbashi, in the south."

Substantial, country-style main dishes followed the hors-d'œuvres. I had ordered a mutton stew. It was served in a polished copper pan, just as it had come out of the oven. It was excellent.

As we enjoyed the meal, I took Dave back to his story of Kisangani. I asked him, "Would you give me a description of your young university?" "Yes, of course, and in fact that's why I invited you two to lunch. At the moment we are only six professors to teach math, physics and chemistry. So far we have not introduced the biological sciences. We hope to next year, in particular botany, as it is very important in that part of the World. For this coming academic year our major problem is physical chemistry. We have nobody who can teach it!"

Margo looked at me with a big smile and I understood what she was thinking. Dave saw her face and said, "Yes, you know what I have in mind — so here goes! Jack, would you be willing to come to teach for the coming academic year?" "I don't know." I replied, "But I'll give it serious thought." Margo's immediate reaction was: "Oh, that would be great". Dave added, "With your B.S. in Chemistry I'm sure, Margo, that I could get you a job as a lab assistant."

Margo had second thoughts, it seemed, as we exchanged questioning looks. We were asking each other, "Would you be willing to do it?"

While we were waiting for the cheese platter, Dave pulled out a collection of photos. They showed typical scenes of life in the Kisangani area, as well as a couple of the 'Fac'. The pictures of the market fascinated Margo, with the people in their native dress.

After the dessert we had coffee, while Dave explained what would be needed for us to be candidates for the posts — if indeed we were interested. He said with confidence, "And I assure you both that you can have the jobs, although the paper work would require a bit of time."

"Yes, Dave, we will think seriously about your proposition. By the way, how did you happen to think of us?" I knew the answer, but awaited his reply. "I've known Marie Josik for many years. When I saw her the day before your lecture, I explained the need for a physical chemist in the Zaïre and asked if she could suggest someone. She immediately mentioned you and Margo, and said that you might possibly be available this coming academic year." As we got up from the table, I noticed that Dave had not touched his glass of wine. "Too bad," I thought, "Such a good Médoc."

We expressed our thanks to Dave for his offer and for the very enjoyable meal. He handed us a card with the 'coordinates' of the hotel where he was staying and urged us to contact him when we had reached a decision concerning the 'Congo adventure'. We shook hands, wished him a good stay in Paris and took a bus back to spend the last night in our hotel room. Along the way back we talked about the future. We stopped at a little bookstore and bought a map of Africa.

Back at the hotel we looked at the huge continent. Right there, dead center, we found Kisangani, with 'Stanleyville' in parenthesis. Margo said, "It's strange, but my mother talked a lot about what she called 'our roots'. I never took it very seriously, as I considered myself to be an American like all the others. My parents had made a big effort to protect me from the problems of segregation." I replied, "I doubt that you could find any traces of your African heritage, above all in the center of the continent. From what I've read the slave trade was primarily along the west coast, here," I said, indicating the region, from Gambia down along the coast to Liberia and Ghana."

We continued our discussion, in particular, of Dave's offer of jobs in Kisangani. In conclusion we agreed that there was nothing to loose by applying. After all, we could always refuse if we got an offer — and had something else that we preferred.

'SOUS LES TOÎTS'

THE NEXT MORNING WE CRAWLED out of bed early, at least for us. Our breakfast arrived a bit later, so we took it standing up. We got everything into the two little suitcases and lugged them downstairs. I paid the bill at the desk and asked the lady to call a taxi for us.

At number four on 'our' little street we saw Mme. Amat in the doorway. "Bonjour, Madame," I called, as we got out of the taxi. The driver offered to carry one suitcase upstairs, for which he was rewarded with an appropriate tip.

We found Gaëtan's little place in good order. We started unpacking our things, as we had forgotten about the two other suitcases — the big ones. Then, there was a knock at the door. I opened it to see a man with a dark-blue cap. "Oh," I said, as I remembered, "Our suitcases." He replied, "Yes, that's right, I have them downstairs. Do you want me to bring them up?" "That would be good, but they are heavy." "They are indeed, but that's my job." It took him at least ten minutes to get them up those three flights, but he succeeded. I handed him a substantial tip, for which he seemed pleased — although he was out of breath.

As we were arranging all our stuff, I thought of Dave's offer. "You know, Margo, to prepare our applications for the Congo, we'll need certified photocopies of a number of documents. For you, your birth certificate and diplomas from Hayward should be enough. But, I'll have to put together a curriculum vitae, as well as the other things. I think that we'll need Marie's help for all that."

With those thoughts, we decided that it was time to eat. As we had nothing in the little apartment, we went down and around the corner to the café where we had met Gaëtan. With a 'croque monsieur' and a little carafe of wine, we were ready to continue. We bought some provisions for the evening at the charcuterie identified by the crying pig, but were at a loss to find something like a supermarket.

When we returned to number four we were greeted by Mme. Amat. In response to our questions, she replied, "But here you have everything: the boulangerie on the corner, the charcuterie that you have apparently already found, and down the street you'll find the 'boucherie' and an 'épicerie'. For the household things, you see down there across the street, there is a 'droguerie'. And, most important, tomorrow morning the market will be here, all along the street. But you'll need a 'filet'." Although I understood all the words, I was lost. She ran back into her little place and came back with a sort of knit bag. She added, "You will need this tomorrow for the market, but later on you can buy one at the droguerie."

That evening we ate what we had bought at the charcuterie and the delicious bread, long, thin loaves, called 'ficelles' (literally, strings). One dish that we had never tasted was 'céleri rémoulade'. We learned that the grated celery was in fact from the large roots of a variety that we had not known. The sauce was distinctive, a mayonnaise with a good dose of mustard.

The next morning we went down stairs and opened the door to the street. The market was animated, to say the least. It was obviously the Sunday morning 'fête'. No doubt for many it was more important than the mass in the church on the corner.

The street was lined with a varied collection of stands. Most were displaying vegetables and fruits on crates or improvised tables. At others there was clothing or knick-knacks of all sorts. There were several stands devoted to ham, sausages and other meat products. All were out in the open to be enjoyed by flies and other insects, and to be contaminated by the dirt of the street and the passersby.

We were walking along the crowded sidewalk when Margo said, "I can already smell it. What is called, a 'pissotière'?"2* As we approached, a client was coming out, just buttoning his fly. He was a little man of an uncertain age, wearing a dark blue beret. He had his just-bought nude baguette under his arm. "What a perfect subject for a poster," I remarked, rather cynically. On the other hand, I reflected, "Maybe we Americans go to far with this question of hygiene. Perhaps our systems get used to living in a disinfected environment and become less able to fight off infection." I was thinking of the motels, with the drinking cups in plastic and the paper-protected toilet seats.

With those thoughts we went ahead and filled our filet, as the other inhabitants of our neighborhood were doing. At each stand we had to ask for the items we wanted and were never allowed to touch. It was not at all a question of hygiene, but just the vendors didn't want their produce injured by indelicate hands. Also, a rotten fruit or vegetable could often be slipped into the lot. The chosen items were weighed with a primitive balance. It consisted of a stick with a string attached to a basket at each end, supported by another string in the middle that the vendor held while he added unmarked weights to compensate for the weight of the purchase. We had to admit that marketing was very different here from that in a U.S. supermarket. By the end of our shopping expedition I had a pocket full of loose change — an indication that we didn't always understand the amount or recognize the coins.

Back 'home' after the long climb upstairs, we prepared our first Sunday dinner together. We decided that we had work to do to develop our culinary skills, although I had had a bit of batching experience.

In the afternoon we took a long walk down Avenue du Général Leclerc. Mme. Amat had told us that his troops lead the Allied Forces into Paris in 1944. At Porte d'Orléans we stopped to watch a soccer match. We were surprised at the violence, particularly on the part of the fans, for a 'no-contact' sport. Across from the Cité Universitaire we entered Parc Monsouris, where we had a very enjoyable visit. After a return home via back streets, we were only able to collapse on the bed.

ANOTHER DECISION

IT WAS MONDAY MORNING. I saw Margo to the Métro station, where she looked at the map to check the way to the Alliance. I saw her off and went to the café on the corner to telephone Marie. I asked if I could see her concerning Dr. Livingston's offer. She replied immediately, "But of course, I'll be in my office all morning." I thanked her and took the Métro to Place Jussieu. From there it was just around the corner to the old chemistry building.

I tapped on the door to the office and entered on Janine's, "Entrez". I said, "Bonjour, Janine" and saw the door to Marie's office open. She called, "Come on in, Jack. Please have a seat. Now, tell me what's on your mind." Marie was, as always, directly to the point. After a pause she continued.

"So now, Young Man, what are your plans for the future?" I hesitated, afraid to admit to her — or to myself — that in fact I had none. She immediately asked, "Do you have an interest in a permanent university position in France?" That one I could answer immediately. "Yes, indeed I do", I replied. "Well, here's the story", she continued. There is a professor in molecular spectroscopy at the University of Bordeaux who will be retiring one of these days. It would normally be at the end of this coming September. However, he has requested an additional year of teaching, which will probably be accorded by the 'Education Nationale'. I think you would have an excellent chance to be named at Bordeaux following his retirement. Furthermore, the lab down there is 'top level' — very well equipped. However, it needs some support on the theoretical side. I think you have the 'baggage' to fill that gap."

"Yes, Marie, I am very much interested in the post but I am not a theoretician." "Yes, I know, but when we say 'theory' in French we mean able to make quantitative interpretation of experimental data." "OK, I understand. What must I do to apply for the post? I don't know anything about the procedures in France." She looked at me as if she were talking to a small boy. "Of course you don't, but we can help you. Janine is very familiar with these things, but you will have to do the initial work, namely, to translate your CV into French." I suddenly had that sinking feeling as I replied, "But I have never studied French, so my knowledge of grammar and spelling is nil." She immediately reassured me with, "Don't worry about it. Just write your CV in your French and Janine will put it all in order."

I went back over what Marie had just said and stopped when I thought of the possibility that the post in Bordeaux might not be available until the following year. Marie read my mind. "I had a long talk last week with our mutual friend, Dave Livingston. He is very anxious for you and Margo to come to the Zaïre. He desperately needs you there. That could be what you might call a stop-gap measure." She had used the expression, 'bouche trou', which seemed very appropriate under the circumstances.

I thanked Marie profusely for her counsel and promised to do my 'homework' as soon as possible. I said, "À bientôt, Marie", as I stepped out next to Janine's desk. "Yes, I know, we are going to put together your dossier for Bordeaux. When you come back with the rough draft of your CV, I'll find out what documents you'll need. Just offhand, they will include your birth certificate, passport, diplomas, and a list of all your scientific publications. I can make certified copies of all, including any others that may be necessary. By the way, Marie told me to make everything in duplicate so that Dr. Livingston can have a copy." I listened to her explanation before remarking, "You know, Janine, your boss is fantastic — what organization!" "Oh yes, that I know well", she said with a big smile.

Margo beat me back home. She had done some shopping on the way and served a nice lunch from what she had bought. That afternoon I dug my little Olivetti out of the bottom of one of the big suitcases and started typing. It was primarily the summary of my research projects, a couple of pages that had to be translated. I went ahead, sentence by sentence, searching always for the various accent marks. I thought, "French can be complicated." I found that the other documents could be used with only minor changes.

I worked all afternoon with numerous references to my inadequate English-French dictionary. Margo read my effort and, although she was making rapid progress, her French was not as yet of much help.

The next morning I went back to see Janine. She scanned my little typescript and said, "Good, now we need to go through it together. I can smooth the French a bit, but you will have to help me with the science. We read it together while she marked the corrections. After an hour or so we had finished and she said that she would retype the summary. She suggested that I come back the following morning so that we could prepare the copies.

On the way back home I stopped in a café and telephoned Dave. He was overjoyed to hear from me and when I said that we were interested in the jobs in the Zaïre, he exclaimed, "That is indeed good news. You know, Jack, we need you desperately down there." "Yes," I answered, "That's exactly what Marie said — that is, Mlle. Josik." He laughed and replied, "You know now that we were in cahoots. Marie said that she could perhaps help me catch you guys!" "You did indeed," I replied. "We'll contact you again in a few days — when the dossiers are ready." "That will be great," he said, "But if you could get them to me by the end of the week it would be good for all concernted. I'll be leaving Paris on Monday."

Margo and I discussed the day's developments. "But why," asked Margo, "Does Marie have an interest in our going to Africa?" After a moment I replied, "I think maybe that it's related to the post in Bordeaux. She thinks that I have enough background in applied math to help the lab there and she is sure that the post will not be available for another year. However, what worries me is the prospect of abandoning my research for a year."

"And what about me," asked Margo. "What could I do in Bordeaux?" "Why it would be perfect for you; you could work for your doctorate. I'm sure you could get an Assistantship," I responded. "Well, maybe," she said with a shrug. There was not much enthusiasm there.

The next morning we continued the routine. Margo went off to her French class and I to work with Janine on the dossiers. By Friday morning, thanks to her efficiency, Janine presented me with the completed documents. I was particularly impressed by the many stamps with squiggly signatures that were everywhere. She said, "I followed Marie's suggestions for the preparation of these certified copies, including the stamps. She told me that administrators, particularly in Africa, are always impressed by them." I thanked Janine for all her work and on the way home stopped to phone Dave. He was very happy with my news and suggested that we meet the following afternoon at four o'clock at the 'Café de la Paix', Rue Aubert. Even I had heard of that place.

It was Saturday afternoon when Margo and I came up from the Métro at the Opéra station. I asked Margo, "Did you see all those legs? I have the impression that all the young ladies are just legs and hair." She giggled and replied, "Do you mean that the skirts are that short?" "No, I didn't mean what you're thinking." She looked at me seriously and remarked, "I have very nice legs, as you may have noticed, but I can't do anything about my hair."

I tried to change the subject. "Here we are. Do you want to go to the Opéra?" "Not really," She replied. "In any case it's not the season." On our left we saw the terrace of the Café de la Paix. Among the number of other Americans, we saw Dave. He greeted us with a wave and indicated a couple of chairs at his table.

The garçon approached, so Margo ordered a Dubonnet. I decided on a beer, as in my student days, "Un demi, s'il vous plaît." I asked Margo, "Where did you learn about Dubonnet?" She countered with, "But it's advertised everywhere here. And how did you know the expression, 'un demi' for a draught of beer?" Touché.

And then, down to serious business, as I handed Dave two folders with our respective dossiers. He gave them a quick look and replied, "They appear to be in excellent form. Please convey my thanks to Janine." We all laughed at that one, as we had arrived at an understanding of the situation.

We finished our 'apéros' and said our goodbyes. Dave hesitated a moment, then pointed out that if we accepted his proposition, we would have to get visas and plane tickets through the Zaïre embassy. "Don't forget, these things may take some time. You'll see, I hope, how it goes in Africa." With that Dave walked off toward his hotel. I noticed that he had left a big bill on the table — enough to cover the drinks and a sizable tip. "Wow," I exclaimed, "This place is expensive. Let's get out of here!"

On the way home I reminded Margo that I had my seminar to prepare for Thursday. "Oh, that's right I had forgotten." "Me too," I responded, "We were so preoccupied with the preparation of those dossiers. I'll phone Marie about the seminar."

On Monday morning we walked down to the Alésia station and Margo left for her French class. I came back to the café on the corner and phoned Marie. In reply to my question she replied, "Yes, My Dear Friend, you do indeed have a talk Thursday afteroon. We can go out to the lab as we did before." So I could look forward to another freightening venture in the lady's deux chevaux.

When Thursday came, I took the Métro to Place Jussieu and walked over to the old building. Marie was in her office ready to go. We took off through the mad Paris triffic and, somehow, arrived at the CNRS lab without incident. After checking my second set of slides, I gave my lecture. I thought it went well and so did Marie. I did notice, however, that many in the audiance appeared to be lost. Marie remarked that the level of math for those who had studied chemistry was not as high as that she had seen in the US.

After the seminar Marie drove me back to Paris. On the way she spoke of the post in Bordeaux and explained. "Now that your dossier is in order, I can push it through the 'Commission' in Paris. I am quite optimistic, but you need to make a personal contact in Bordeaux. Before Bastille Day, only a couple of weeks away, you ought to make a trip down there. Let me know when you could go and I'll arrange for you to be taken care of there for a day or two." Of course I agreed and indicated that I could make the trip whenever it was convenient for the group there.

When I phoned the next morning, Janine answered. She immediately asked, "Can you go to Bordeaux on Monday?" "Sure, there's no problem." She went on to say that I should pick up my ticket at the Gare d'Austerlitz for the train at 8:47. The trip would take approximately six hours and

I would be met on arrival by Professor Lesquin, who is the Assistant Director of the lab down there. I thanked Janine once again for her help and assured her that I would catch the train.

That afternoon I asked Margo if she had an interest in making the trip to Bordeaux. "No, not at all. I'm really not inspired by Bordeaux. Besides I have my French classes. I can't afford to miss any, as we have an exam coming up before the vacation."

BORDEAUX

So, ON MONDAY MORNING I crawled out of bed very early, said goodbye to Margo and arrived at the Gare around eight o'clock to pick up my ticket. I found the right platform without too much trouble. There, a man in a white jacket was taking reservations for lunch. That was what I called 'looking ahead'. I found the seat that I had reserved, again in a compartment with six places. The train pulled out at exactly 8:47. Although it was a purely business trip, I was able to see a lot of the French countryside. After leaving the Paris area it was a continuous farm to Orleans, the first stop.

There was virtually no communication between the various passengers in the compartment until the train stopped at Orleans. There, a lady got on with two small children. Suddenly, there was activity. The kids talked to everybody. One gent, probably German, when addressed by the two children was able to trot out a few sentences in French. I made friends with the two little guys, but found that their French was difficult to understand. I imagine that the linguistic problem with children is similar in any society. The little family got off when we stopped for a couple of minutes at Blois. From the train I got just a glimpse of the famous château.

When the man in the white jacket came down the corridor ringing his little bell, it was time for lunch. I went down to the Wagon Restaurant, were I was seated at an elegant table — white tablecloth, polished silver, and a bottle of Listrac. There was a middle-aged English couple already seated, tourists on the way to Spain. We chatted all through the meal. It was served in much the same style as I had seen on board ship, although with much haste.

After the stop at Angoulême the countryside was all vineyards. They were in seemingly infinite rows stretching into the distance. From

Libourne it was only a short ride until I could see the skyline of Bordeaux, with the harbor in the foreground. We crossed the Garonne and I got off with my attaché-case at Gare Saint Jean. I was immediately met by a monsieur who identified himself as James Lesquin. "I'm pleased to meet you," my name is Jacques Gilbert; but how did you know who I was?" He laughed and answered, "I attended your lecture a couple of years ago at a Gordon Conference. We didn't actually meet, although I think that it was there that you made the acquaintance of Marie Josik. She directed my thesis work a number of years ago."

James and I took a bus to Place de la Victoire with its arch — a small version of the Arc de Triomphe in Paris. While we were waiting for another bus I asked James how he happened to have an English first name. He explained that there were still vestiges of the period when the region was occupied by the English. He added that they were finally chased out after the Battle of Castillon in 1453. "That's amazing", I remarked, "That there are still traces of their occupation after so long a time."

When the 'G' bus arrived we took it for a few minutes to the suburb of Talence. We got off the bus near a gateway, the entrance to the campus. There were buildings at either side of a pond surrounded by trees and a lawn covered with mushrooms. James explained, "The campus is quite recent, as all of the buildings are only a few years old. Before, this was one of the most important vineyards in France. You can imagine the value of the land!" "Well, yes," I responded. "And by the way, are the mushrooms edible?" "Yes," he replied, "But they are not very tasty, so nobody bothers to pick them."

We entered one of the buildings and took the elevator to the top floor. James remarked, "We are just in time for tea." That seemed a bit strange to me; and, just as we entered and walked down the hall I heard the announcement on the intercom, "Le thé est prêt." It gave me the occasion to meet many of the members of the Lab, although I could not assimilate all their names. I did notice, however, that there was more than tea. There was coffee, of course, but also a number of opened bottles of wine. In response to my glance in their direction, James said, "Oh yes, we have the 'Laboratoire d'Œnologie' just downstairs." That one stopped me. Everybody laughed before James explained, "Œnologie refers to the science of wine making. The Lab down there receives many bottles for testing and, once a small sample has been removed, we get some of what is left."

After the 'tea' session James lead me down the hall. He tapped at a door marked, 'Professeur J. ROBIN, Directeur.' We entered on his "Entrez". The office was very large, with big windows overlooking the campus. Professor Robin, a balding gentleman with rimless glasses, sat behind his big desk. He was waring a suit and tie and somehow gave the impression of having nothing to do. I knew that he had abandoned research some years before to devote himself to administration and the required teaching, but, as far as the lab was concerned, it seemed that James was the boss.

I shook hands with Monsieur Robin, who wished me a pleasant visit in Bordeaux and talked a bit about the attractions of the region. He admitted that he had become tired of teaching after so many years and was looking forward to retirement in another year. I had the feeling that this information was for my benefit.

We left the office and made a tour of the Lab. I was suitably impressed by the collection of up-to-date scientific instruments. James proudly presented a new spectrometer, which he described as, "The first commercial Laser-Raman instrument in the World. It was designed and built in Paris." For a moment I thought back to an exchange that I had with my young colleague, Ben, at the Research Center. It was the morning when the discovery of the Laser had been announced — and just before Ben's untimely death.

After the visit to the lab James and I walked out through the gate and turned down the Cours de la Libération to a small restaurant. James indicated that there was a hotel upstairs where he had reserved a room for me. He said that he was sorry that he was busy for the evening and asked if he could come by for me the next morning around nine. "We have planned a visit to the nearby CNRS lab tomorrow morning and have been invited to lunch with the Director. We know that you have a train in the afternoon, but we will see that you catch it." He added that the little restaurant was not fancy, but quite acceptable, and wished me a pleasant evening.

The next morning we walked back to the campus. We found his car, certainly a cut above Marie's, and in five minutes approached what appeared to be a country club. In front of the laboratory building were a couple of horses and a barn behind a rail fence, as well as a tennis court. James explained that the Director was a tennis buff, but that it was his wife who insisted on the horses.

Inside the building it was like any other modern research lab. As we walked down the hall, a rather tall, athletic-looking man came out a door and jogged down to meet us. James introduced him as Monsieur Renaud, Director of the lab. He greeted me with "I'm very glad to meet you, Professor Gilbert. I saw you and James from the window. James will give you a little tour of the lab and then I hope you will join us for lunch." "With pleasure," I replied.

The Lab reminded me very much of the CNRS lab where I had given my talks. It was very well equipped with recent instruments and an apparently friendly team of researchers. James explained that there was very close cooperation with the University lab that we had visited the afternoon before. He went on to say that he expected to assume the directorship of the Lab at the Fac, although Professor Robin's University position will be vacant upon his retirement. He added, "I suspect that Marie has told you these things," "Yes, she has," I replied, "And as you no doubt suspect, that's why I made the trip to Bordeaux." "Yes, I know, and I think that you would be very welcome here."

At lunchtime James lead me to a door near Monsieur Renaud's office. He tapped and entered what was in effect a private apartment. Mme. Renaud greeted me and her husband introduced two visitors, a Pole and a Belgian. After a round of apéros we were seated and served an excellent family-style meal. The 'plat de résistance' was 'lapin aux pruneaux' (rabbit with prunes), a regional specialty.

After lunch James looked at his watch and remarked, "Jacques, we have to be off if you want to catch your train." We left the lunch group with a hasty goodbye and headed out to James' car. It was then a rather frantic ride to Gare Saint Jean — but we had five minutes to spare.

The return to Paris was uneventful but long. It was followed by the

Métro to Alésia. I found Margo studying her French. She said that she had already eaten, but there was bread and cheese — and a half-bottle of wine on the table. She asked about Bordeaux, to which I replied, "I really saw nothing but scientific stuff, although on the way to the train station James did talk briefly about the area. He spoke of the Coast and Arcachon, as well as the interior — the Dordogne. I noticed at the time that he made no mention of the City of Bordeaux." Margo had no apparent reaction.

I continued, "For us, the future appears to be more-or-less defined. It is clear that I am expected to be named to the post at Bordeaux. Furthermore, Professor Robin will not be retiring until next year. So, from what has been said it seems certain that we will be going to the Zaïre this fall. What do you think of that?" She replied, "OK, I really do want to go to Africa." As for Bordeaux, she had no comment.

Later in the week we went by to see Marie and give her a summary of my trip to Bordeaux. She responded with, "I think now that your situation is in order. I have no doubt that you will be named to the post in Bordeaux next year. As for the Zaïre, there too, I have confidence in Dave. But," she added, "You'll have to be patient." We nodded with understanding as she went on to say, "Now all you two have to do is to visit Paris and get your things in order for your trip to Africa. Don't hesitate to contact me if you need any help. I'm off on vacation at the end of the week, but I'll be back in mid-August, as I have work to do for the meeting." We replied with our many thanks and, "Bonnes vacances, Marie."

SUMMER TOURIST

BACK HOME IN OUR LITTLE studio we started planning our touristic attack on Paris. I got out the Michelin and we made a little list of things to do and see.

Tour Eiffel,

Champs-Elysées,

Montmartre,

Louvre,

Place Pigalle (by night),

Isle de la Cité (Sainte Chapelle, Conciergerie),

Place Vendôme, Quartier Juif,

Bois de Boulogne, Versailles, Jardin et Zoo de Vincennes

— Chartres, Fontainebleau, Châteaux de la Loire, ...

Each day we chose our project from the list. Along the way to our destination we walked through different neighborhoods just to get a taste of everyday Paris. As we passed the windows along the sidewalk, we often saw a cat lying on a ledge in the sun in front of the white curtains. These creatures suggested calm and contentment.

The real curiosity was to be seen a floor or two higher. Often there was a lady of a certain age sitting in the window. She seemed to be completely absorbed in watching the passersby. That in itself was hardly surprising, but we had to laugh when we saw two mirrors, like rear-view mirrors on a car. They were mounted on the outside at either side of the window so that the lady could watch the comings and goings far down the sidewalk.

In the evening Margo and I often discussed what we had seen during the day and compared our reactions. It was immediately apparent that we didn't have the same ideas. Our appreciation was often different. In general Margo preferred the current scene, the Tour Eiffel, the Champs-Elysées, while I was particularly impressed by the Conciergerie and its history. However, after our daylong hike up the hill to Sacré Cœur, we had to agree that Montmartre, with its view and Place du Tertre, was the outstanding visit on our agenda.

Our tourism was interrupted one day when we received a letter from Dave down in the Zaïre. He wrote that my application for the post as Visiting Professor for the coming academic year had been accepted. He expressed surprise that it had been approved so rapidly, but as he had said, they desperately needed someone to teach physical chemistry. He went on to say that we should go right away to the Zaïre Embassy in Paris to ask about our plane tickets.

That evening I typed a letter to the Chemistry Department at Hayword University. I explained that I had accepted an appointment for one year in Kisangani and asked for a year's leave without pay. It seemed logical to be sure of the position in Bordeaux before resigning in Washington.

The next morning we took the Métro to Alma-Marceau. When we came up next to the Seine we looked back and saw in the distance the green flag with an arm and a torch in a circle. We recognized it as the flag of the Zaïre. Inside we identified ourselves and enquired about plane tickets. We were told that we would have to wait, as they had not yet received confirmation from Kinshasa. They suggested that we come back the following week.

Somewhat relieved by the assurance that we would have at least one job in the fall, we went back to our tourism. Margo remarked that she was getting tired of the city, so we decided to go to Versailles. The next morning we took the Métro to the Montparnasse station and found a train for Versailles. There we spent the day 'doing' the whole place. Near the end of the afternoon we discovered 'Le hameau de la Reine', where we were immediately charmed. For us it was a pleasant relief after the over-kill architecture of the Palace and the too-neat Cartesian gardens.

An then it was Bastille day, the fourteenth of July. In the evening we went to the Champs-Elysées. It was swimming with tourists like us. We walked through the crowd with some difficulty, up toward the Arc de Triomphe. Finally, we turned down the avenue de Iéna and could see the Eiffel tower in the distance. As we walked along, I remarked that the avenue was certainly named after the battle, but for me it is written with a 'Ja' in German and is best known for its optical quality glass.

At eleven the sky suddenly burst with fireworks. The impressive display went on for an hour, ending with a most spectacular series of explosions of all colors. Margo said that it reminded her of home on the fourth, although there it is the Washington Monument, rather than the Effel Tower that provides the setting.

The following week we went back to the Zaïre Embassy to inquire about our plane tickets. However, the answer was the same: "Maybe next week." The story was repeated until we realized that mid-August had arrived and that Marie would be back from vacation.

I phoned Marie's office, where Janine answered. After only two words she responded with "Bonjour, Jacques, ça va?" Apparently I had not yet acquired a Parisian accent — and certainly never would. With a brief exchange with Janine I heard Marie on the line. She inquired about Margo, our impressions of Paris and the evolution of our plans — in particular, if we had heard from Dave. She seemed very happy to learn that my post had been assured. She added that she was sure that there was no problem for Margo to have the Assistantship and that we should be patient for the question of plane tickets. She explained, "The time scale is quite different in the 'developing countries'."

While I had Marie on the phone, I said that Dave had urged us to buy a car and have it shipped as soon as possible. "Do you have any idea whom to contact here," I asked? She immediately suggested, "Talk to Janine, she can help you." With that she said goodbye and to hold. Then I heard Janine back on the line. "OK, for a used car, I'll ask my boyfriend. He's a mechanic in a garage near Paris. If you call back tomorrow, I can probably help you." I thanked her and was somewhat relieved by her confidence.

In fact, the following morning Janine responded to my call with the phone number and address of her boyfriend's garage. She said that she had described my plan to go to the Congo for a year and that he had immediately suggested that I buy a Méhari. "What's that," I asked? "Well, you know Marie's deux chevaux," she replied. "Oh yes," I thought. But she went on to say, "It's in effect a 'trois chevaux' but all in plastic. It was designed specifically for use in Africa. I suggest that you talk with Michel." I thanked Janine once again for her help and immediately called Michel and arranged to see him the following morning.

I took the Métro to Porte de Pantin and eventually found a bus to Bobigny, east of Paris. I followed with little difficulty the directions that Michel had given me. The garage was identified by a huge corporal's chevron, the Citroën symbol. Inside, I met Michel, at home in his greasy duds and cheerful greeting. He led me through the vast array of carcasses in all states of disrepair. We stopped beside a kaki-colored vehicle that was suggestive of the Soviet command cars that I had seen in movies. "So here it is," he exclaimed! "It's called a Méhari, after the dromedary in North Africa that is known for its endurance. It's just what you're looking for. Furthermore, I think I can get you a good price. I'll talk to the owner." With that introduction he proceeded to describe the mechanical advantages of this little car.

"And most of all, it can be repaired with just a few hand tools. If you decide to buy it, I can provide you with a kit of tools and spare parts. You don't have to be an automobile mechanic to solve most problems that you are likely to have down there." As I started to worry about shipping the car to Africa, Michel read my mind. He continued with, "We can arrange to have the car driven to our garage in Le Havre and Janine will call about sending it on to Africa."

With some relief I responded that if he could make an estimate of the cost of the whole venture, I'd talk it over with my lady and get back to him. "OK," he answered, "I'll contact the owner about the price and make an estimate of the cost of the tools and parts. Janine will contact the shipping company. I suggest that you go by to see her in a day or two."

Two days later I tapped on the door to Janine's office and entered. She jumped up from behind her desk and came out to greet me with the 'bises' — a little kiss on either cheek! "I have good news", she exclaimed. "Michel says you can have the Méhari for 1400 Frs. He said that if you could add 100 Frs., he'd send a box of tools and spare parts." I realized that Janine was talking in "new francs" had only recently been introduced in France. I thought immediately that for approximately $750 dollars it was difficult to go wrong!

"Wow," I exclaimed, "Your guy is great." Her reply with a big smile was, "Oh, yes, I know that well. By the way I called a company about the shipment from Le Havre. She looked down at a sheet of paper on her desk. They said that it would be sent to the port of Matadi by freighter, then by train to Kinshasa and finally by boat up the Congo River to Kisangani. It sounds terribly complicated, but they promised to get back to me with an estimate of the price." "And you're great, too," I replied.

On my return to home I got out the big map of Africa and traced the route that Janine had explained. When Margo arrived I told her that we now had a car, but it would probably take a long time for it to get to the Zaïre. In any case we weren't there yet!

However, the next day we made our weekly trip to the Embassy and found, rather to our surprise by now, that a document had arrived from Kinshasa. It was a letter of credit for our plane tickets, as well as for all baggage and other items to be shipped. When I asked specifically about the car, the reply was simply, "Yes, of course, all of your expenses for your stay in our country are covered. As for your tickets, they are available at the Havas travel agency on Boulevard Haussemann." We were so astonished we didn't know how to respond. With just our thanks and a handshake we hurried off to pick up our tickets and reserve for our trip into Africa.

That evening we went back to the restaurant where we had eaten with Dave. It was a celebration for the arrival of the tickets, as well as in honor of our car which we had never driven and which Margo hadn't even seen! At the table I asked Margo, "By the way do you have a driver's license?" "Oh, no, I didn't think of that. I took lessons from my father, but I didn't take the exam!"

After dinner we decided to see Paris by night. We took a bus — in fact two of them. Certainly the Métro is not the way to go if you want to see something. When we got off we were at Place Pigalle. What better place to see Paris by night! As I told Margo, the GI's who came through here at the end of the War called it 'Pig Alley'. As we started our little promenade, we saw immediately why it was so named.

Along the walk numerous samples of all sexes were on display. There was often a 'maquereau' in the doorway urging the passersby to enter. Although we were not particularly interested in his products, we were amused by the atmosphere of the neighborhood.

On a little side street a neon sign indicating music identified a little nightclub — a 'boîte de nuit'. "Well, why not," I suggested. "Let's go in to see what it's like." We were welcomed at the door and lead to places near a little stage where a combo, consisting of piano, drums and alto sax, was in action. We took the indicated places and ordered drinks.

The music was really quite good— not too loud and not too nervous. The blind pianist was impressive. At one moment he went into his solo and the sax man picked up a flute and improvised 'noodles'. It was not that different from the classical chamber music that I knew. When Margo remarked that she found the music boring I started thinking about our difference in taste. Maybe because I was twelve years older. Or was it just cultural?

On Monday morning it was the opening of the international meeting that Marie had organized. She had arranged for a minibus to pick up the expected participants at Place Jussieu at nine. My talk was scheduled for that afternoon. At around eight thirty I arrived and saw several of my North-American colleagues already waiting. I was very pleased to see them and to welcome them, as I was a newly established Parisian. "And, hey," someone shouted, "He speaks English!"

Around ten the bus arrived at a small château somewhere near Chartres. When we got off we saw a desk on the lawn and a sign marked 'Registration'. Janine was sitting behind the desk. She jumped up to welcome the group. When she saw me she came up to exchange the bises. Someone behind me with a British-like accent remarked, "Is that the way we are welcomed to this meeting? Extraordinary!"

I had lunch with my colleagues and in the afternoon gave my little talk. It was well received and admittedly, it was a bit easier in English.

Back home with Margo I remarked, "Do you realize the day after tomorrow we are to take the plane?" "Oh yes, I know," she replied. "I've been worrying about it for several days."

And so the next day was devoted to the preparation of our baggage. We stuffed two foot lockers with things to be sent and two suitcases of the essentials for the trip. We had understood that the shipped baggage might take a long time to get there. In fact, we were warned that often all traces of it might be lost. Kinshasa was known for the theft of baggage in transit.

That evening we stopped downstairs to see Mme. Amat. We said that we would be leaving very early the next morning and that we had left two pieces of baggage that would be picked up in a day or two for shipment. She said goodbye to each of us with hugs and kisses. "I have been really so happy to have you young people here", she said. "We too have enjoyed staying here with you and soon you'll have your Canadian back", I replied.

Our alarm clock sounded terribly early the next morning. It was already getting light, but of course it was summer and Europe is further north than one thinks.

When our two suitcases were finally ready and downstairs, I went around to the taxi stand at the café on the corner. I got a cab and gave directions to where Margo was waiting. Our early morning ride to the Orly Airport was rapid, as there was little traffic. With our check-in completed — baggage through to Kinshasa — we had time for our coffee before the plane to Brussels.

When the flight was announced we showed our passports and went through the exit gate. On board we found our seats and saw that the plane was nearly full, mostly with businessmen. A number of them picked up Flemish newspapers and settled down to read while awaiting their morning coffee.

When we were about to take off I noticed that Margo was very quiet. I asked, "Are you OK?" She murmured, "Well, yes, I guess so. But you know, this is the first time I've been on a plane." "I understand," I said,

"But I've only flown once before — if that makes you feel any better!"

We took off, but the descent for Brussels was announced before we had much time to think about it. Once landed we entered the terminal at Zaventem. We were not even legally in Belgium, as we were in transit. We checked for the plane to Kinshasa and were told that there would be a delay. "How long?" I asked. "Maybe a couple of hours or so", was the vague reply. So we had nothing to do but look around at the junk on sale and wait.

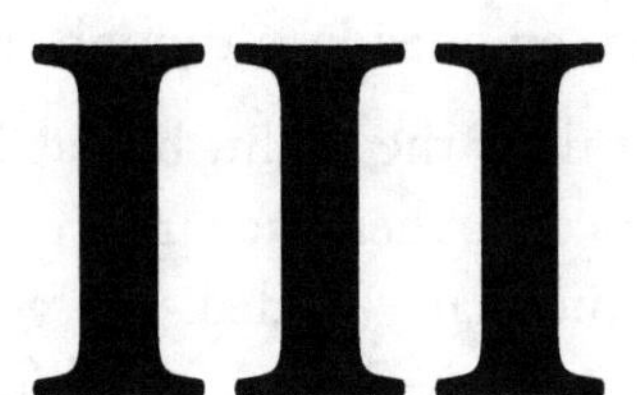

INTO AFRICA

FINALLY, WE WERE SEATED IN the big plane. It was near the end of the afternoon when it took off. The day already seemed long, especially the past five hours in the air terminal. On the plane we were glad to get the standard, plastic-like meal, as we had had little to eat since our coffee on the commuter flight.

As dusk fell, we could just make out the silhouette of the Rock of Gibraltar before we crossed the straits. We were now over the African Continent, but it had turned dark. "Is that symbolic," I asked myself? There was nothing to be seen outside, although sleep was impossible.

The plane droned on into the night, but at last it changed its tune and we could feel the descent. Then the airport of Kinshasa - Ndjili was announced and shortly the plane landed. We got up and followed the crowd down the steps and touched African soil for the first time.

We entered the terminal building, where a man in a rather tattered uniform was at the entrance gate. He took a quick look at our passports and waved us on in. Right behind him stood a relatively well-dressed younger man. As each male passenger came in he asked, "Professeur Gilbert?" "Oui, c'est moi," I exclaimed. He introduced himself as "Jérôme" and explained that he represented the University in Kisangani. He said that he had been sent to welcome us. He immediately led us to a counter where another more-or-less uniformed man was waiting with our two suitcases. Jérôme nodded to him, picked up the two heavy suitcases and led us out of the building. Once outside he explained that an important part of his job was getting us through customs and providing any other aid that we might need. It was then that we understood the 'mitabish' — the palm-greasing principle.

Jérôme loaded our baggage into his beat-up car and we got in. We drove along a narrow paved road, apparently toward the city of Kinshasa. Along the way there was a continuous series of bonfires at the side of the road with groups of men sitting around them. Jérôme explained that they always had fires at night to repel all kinds of beast that might come around. In answer to my question, he said that the very strong, characteristic odor we had noticed came from the wood used in the bonfires.

He stopped the car in front of a rather dilapidated two-story building. We entered, with Jérôme lugging both suitcases. He led us upstairs and indicated a room, equipped with a double bed and a chair. He indicated that there was a toilet down the hall.

Jérôme left us with, "Bonne nuit", although it was five o'clock in the morning. He said that we could get breakfast downstairs and that he would be by later to organize our short visit to Kinshasa.

We collapsed for what was left of the night. But an hour later, the sun came up rather suddenly. We tried to snooze for another hour or so, but finally gave up and went down to breakfast.

At our places along a big table we were immediately welcomed by an American lady — judging from her accent. Within a few minutes she brought us a big, American-style breakfast, with bacon and eggs, toast and watery coffee. Then, suddenly everyone at the table joined hands and somebody said a short prayer. We finally realized that we were in a Protestant Mission.

After breakfast we went out onto the street. It was lined with run-down houses, but little other signs of habitation. As a young man came shuffling along the street, I asked him where was the center of the city. He replied, "C'est ici, it is here; you are in the center of Kinshasa". Difficult to imagine, but later on the morning with the help of Jérôme, we discovered a bit more of what we had thought a city should look like. However, we then began to change some of our ideas from what we had known in Europe and America.

Jérôme said that we had an administrative matter to tend to. He reminded us to have our passports and visas and then took us to a section of the city where there were several buildings. We entered an office that was the Immigration Service and presented our documents.

Jérôme immediately disappeared behind, but returned within a couple of minutes. The man behind the counter nodded to him and immediately stamped our documents with various official-looking names and symbols. He then took them to the office behind. He returned shortly and we saw that each stamp had been adorned with an unreadable signature.

Back in the car I asked Jérôme about the procedure in the office. He explained, "Oh, it's just like with Customs last night. The University provides me with a budget so that the various formalities can be accomplished with a minimum of difficulty. In this country it is what you would probably call 'standard procedure'." The last two words he said in English with but little accent.

"Now that we have the papers in order, would you like to eat," Jérôme asked? "Oh, no," we responded simultaneously, "We just ate a huge, American-style breakfast." "Then, would you join me for something to drink? It's already getting hot." "Sure," we replied, "That's a good idea." Jérôme led us into a café and we were seated. He waited to see what we ordered before he made another comment. After we had both ordered beer (It was Primus, of course), he remarked, "I was waiting to see if you were like most of the Missionaries, 'teetotalers', as they say." "No," I responded, "We are not Missionaries — and most certainly not teetotalers!"

We told Jérôme about our backgrounds as chemists and our reasons for coming to Africa. In turn, he gave us a short history of the University in Kisangani and explained the contributions of the various Protestant groups in several countries. He explained that we would find the Staff composed of people from all over the World.

After the very informative chat with Jérôme, he drove us to our Mission. He said that we could get dinner there. As we were thanking him for his help, he said, "And now for the remaining problem, I'll pick you up early, say seven thirty, tomorrow morning. I'll try to get you places on the plane to Kisangani.

That evening we ate a very simple dinner. We noticed that there was no trace of an alcoholic beverage, thus confirming Jérôme's remarks. We went immediately to bed, as we had not recovered from the long trip.

We were waiting for Jérôme as he drove up at exactly seven thirty. The ride to the airport was the inverse of what we had done the night of our arrival, but the effect was not at all the same. There were many people walking along the road. Now there were many women in brightly colored dresses or, sometimes, just wrapped in strips of cloth —'Dutch wax', as Jérôme called the tissue.

At the airport terminal Jérôme said, "Just wait here and I'll see what I can do." We now understood the procedure. Jérôme disappeared behind the counter, this time for some minutes. When he came back we saw another, apparently important man coming out from the back office. He came up beside the man at the counter, picked up the clipboard and, apparently at random, scratched off two names on the passenger list. We overheard him say, "There are two places for Professeur and Madame." He made a sign to Jérôme and disappeared.

Jérôme showed us to the waiting room and said, "Now all you have to do is wait until your plane to Kisangani is announced. That should be in an hour or so, but one never knows." He left us with our many thanks for all his help. He said that he had errands to do, as he was expecting another University person on the evening flight from Brussels.

About an hour later our plane was announced. A number of people stood up and we moved with them out across the airfield to a small plane, a Fokker, with an upper wing and two props. Inside, we found our places immediately behind the two pilots. They were white and speaking English. I counted twelve passengers. After a bit, one of the pilots picked up a microphone and announced in French that we should land in Kisangani in about four hours. The plane took off and we were on our way — so we thought.

As we were circling the city, we saw a large body of water, the Congo River, and across in the distance some buildings. That was Brazzaville, in the 'other' Congo. (We had been told that we couldn't go there with American passports.)

Soon, one of the pilots switched on the radar. We could see the screen in front of us. It displayed a series of horizontal lines, then flickered a number of times and finally turned to snow. After a minute or two of playing with knobs on the dashboard, the copilot threw up his hands. As the plane banked sharply, he announced that we would be returning to Kinshasa 'for technical reasons'.

We landed and trouped out across the airfield to the terminal building. There, we were offered coffee and a sandwich. An hour or so later the plane for Kisangani was again announced. Back on the plane the takeoff was as before. Then, the copilot turned on the radar and the scenario was repeated! The other passengers couldn't see the radar screen and nothing was said about the problem. I heard the pilot say in English, "Oh well, it doesn't matter; we'll just follow the river."

As the afternoon went on, we got acquainted with a young African sitting across the aisle. He said that he was a student in Kisangani and that he had been down in Kinshasa to visit his parents. At one moment he looked at his watch and said, "We should make it. You know (we didn't), we have to get to Kisangani by six, as there are no lights on the airfield there." He didn't seem to be the slightest bit worried about the situation.

From the window we could see the river, with a continuous carpet of green forest on either side. It was only occasional marked by a tiny clearing near the river. From time-to-time we could see an object in the water — either a very little boat or a very big crocodile.

After several hours of flight the copilot pushed a button on the dashboard and there was music. It provided the atmosphere for arrival — African drums on a string background. We felt the plane slowing down and turning left with a sharp bank. We came in so low over the river that we had the impression that we were 'landing' in the water. Then suddenly, land appeared just under us and we touched down on the bank of the river. The applause by the dozen passengers was definitely appropriate in this case. We tried not to imagine what it would have been like after dark.

KISANGANI (STANLEYVILLE)

WE CAME OUT OF THE plane and stepped down onto the airfield. There, waiting, was a white man whom I recognized as Dave Livingston. We walked toward each other and, as we shook hands, I said, "Doctor Livingston, I presume. Strange that we should meet here." He burst out laughing and exchanged bises with Margo — à la française. I asked if he had been waiting long, as the plane was several hours late. He replied, "No, we had heard that there was a delay." "Oh, did Jérôme telephone,"

I asked? "Telephone? No, they are very rare around here. The drums told us." As we both looked quizzically at Dave, he went on to explain. Each time that the plane passed over a village, the message was sent on. A sort of Morse code on the drums, based on the spoken language. It had said, 'The big, noisy bird just passed.' "I don't understand the drums, but Samuel, our assistant at the Fac, does. He keeps us up-to-date on the news. Of course the messages travel with the speed of sound, so we heard of your arrival from a village down the river well before you got here. And now, I imagine that you're hungry. Inga is waiting for us with a bit of supper."

As we walked toward a car, the only one in sight, it suddenly turned dark. It was as if somebody had just switched off the lights. Dave laughed, "Yes, we are almost on the Equator here. You know immediately when it's six o'clock. Tomorrow morning you'll see the inverse effect at exactly six AM."

As we were driving to his house, Dave said that a nice house had been reserved for us near the Fac, but there was no use going to see it until tomorrow morning. 'We have a spare room, as our daughter is back in the States for her studies. This is her freshman year at Ohio State." Dave continued to talk of his daughter as we drove along. He said that she had especially enjoyed her visit to Kisangani this past summer.

Dave stopped the car. The only light to be seen was from a little bonfire. There was the silhouette of a figure before it. Dave remarked, "He's our 'vigil'; he's paid to pass the night there. In principle it's to protect us from intruders, but in fact it's primarily to give him a little job. We all help the local economy by hiring several people, gardeners, 'house boys', etc. Incidentally, when you take on servants in the house, it's preferable to avoid the term 'boy', as it's considered to be pejorative.

The door to the house opened and Inga was standing in the doorway, the bright lights of the interior behind her. Dave presented his wife, who was an attractive lady — in her forties I guessed. She greeted us with, "You must be famished; please be seated." She indicated places at the table, that was already set and awaiting our arrival.

When we were seated, Inga rang a little bell that was on the table before her. Immediately, the domestic entered with a big dish of meatballs and a bowl of plain, boiled potatoes. Dave then indicated that we should join hands while he said the prayer. It was the same ceremony that we had witnessed at the Mission in Kinshasa. Here again there was no sign of any alcoholic beverage. I then understood why Dave had left his Médoc untouched in the restaurant in Paris.

The next morning after breakfast Dave said that he had work to do at the Fac and that Inga would show us our house. We followed Inga out to the car, a Peugeot 204. I remarked, "Oh, you have a French car." "Yes," she replied, "Dave bought it in Paris and had it shipped." "We have done the same thing, but ours is a Méhari. Sort of the French answer to the Jeep. How long did yours take to get here?" "About three months," she answered. "Then I guess we have about two more months to wait."

After only a short drive we stopped in front of a little one-story house. It had several palm trees in front and was surrounded by a lawn. Inga unlocked the grillwork in front of the entrance and we came into a neat living room and a dining area with a table and several chairs. The furniture was all in hard wood. Inga remarked that it had all been hand-made in the University shops. The living room was simply furnished with two armchairs, a bookcase and a lamp. Behind the dining area was a little kitchen, with a table, a stove and a small refrigerator. There was a door that opened onto a grassy back yard, with a small stream running by and several very tall palm trees.

Returning to the living room, Inga opened a door that lead to a hall, with a bedroom at each side. She indicated that it was good to have a spare bedroom in case we had visitors — hardly expected in our case. There was a small, but completely equipped bathroom. "Very rare here," Inga said.

The floor throughout the house was tiled. I noticed that it had turned black in a large area in the living room, only partially hidden by small carpets. Inga laughed and explained, "This house was used by the military during the Simba revolt. The soldiers of course lit fires inside the house. After the occupation of Kisangani the University recovered a number of houses and fixed them up for use by the teachers. Incidentally, this particular house was one of the better ones. It belonged to the chief brewer here. The brewery was the principle establishment in Belgian times."

As we went back to the car we both said that we were pleased with the house. It was certainly much better than we had expected.

Inga drove us into what she described as, 'The center of town'. There were several one-story buildings, all in very bad shape. What probably had once been windows were boarded up. Most of the walls were pockmarked by bullets. The few people in the streets were mostly men in very old clothes — rags, from our point of view. Many were bare footed. We saw no cars other than our own.

We parked in front of an unidentified shop. It was boarded-up and quite dim inside. The proprietor was fairly light-skinned, probably an Indian. There were piles of canned goods, sacks of flour and pasta, and a few baskets of produce, in particular, leeks and sweet potatoes. We saw loaves of bread in big paper bags and boxes of UHT milk, but no other diary products. A few items caught our attention: cartons of canned sardines and tomato paste, and, on a high shelf, jugs of Portuguese wine! Then I spotted some little cans in a far corner. They were of Russian caviar. I asked the proprietor about these apparently strange items. He explained, "Oh, well, those were ordered by the Russians who came into the country for a short time. By the time the stuff got here, the Russians were gone and nobody has ever bought any." I promised to help him get rid of his stock.

We bought a few things, including bread and wine, but no caviar this time. Inga went on to explain that there were two other ways to go. Either you went to the native market, where you will find the local products, or you wait for the arrival of the 'Grey ghost'. "What," I asked, "is the Grey ghost?" Inga replied, "It's our nickname for the airplane that arrives every month to provide produce for the missionaries here. It brings all sorts of things that many of us find missing in our every-day life." I made no comment, as I decided to wait to see what the local market had to offer.

Inga led us out of the shop and along the street. I noticed, in particular, a man sitting on a low stool. He was working with a small sewing machine perched on a crate. It was a 'Singer' that was hand-operated by turning a little crank. He was a tailor who made and, much more often, tried to repair clothing. A bit further down the street we entered a little butcher shop. As Inga said, "The stock is limited, but at least I have the impression that it is more-or-less refrigerated." We saw lots of chicken and pork, but only a few pieces of mutton and beef. Inga indicated that beef was very expensive, as it was all imported.

We came back to our new home and deposited our purchases. Inga showed us around in more detail. She said that the bedding was for us until our things arrived. But she added, "Don't hold your breath, that stuff may take a long time to get here." She went out with, "Dave said it would be good for you to come to the Fac tomorrow morning so that he can show you around and present you to your colleagues." With that she went on her way and we set out to fix our first meal 'chez nous'.

At one point in the morning there was a tap on the kitchen door. We opened it to find a lady in the usual attire, holding a wooden object rather like a big rolling pin. She said that she had come to welcome us as new neighbors and, following the local tradition, to give us a present. She explained that the object in question was a pestle, used in the preparation of various foods. I couldn't help thinking that it looked even more dangerous than a rolling pin, the traditional wifely weapon.

After lunch we tried out the new bed. It was very welcome after the long trip into Africa. However, in our haste to get to bed we hadn't noticed that there were no curtains or shades on the windows. In fact there was no glass either, just screens to discourage the local mosquitoes. When we woke up after our siesta, it was still daylight outside. At the window we saw a row of little pairs of eyes staring at us. If they were there when we went to bed, we wouldn't have noticed — but the kids must have had a good show.

THE 'FAC'

The next morning we walked along what appeared to be a main road, following the directions that Inga had given us. There were a few houses along the way, most in a state of serious disrepair. After about fifteen minutes we arrived at a one-story building marked with a sign in front, 'Université Nationale du Zaïre'. We entered and found a small office where a young man was seated behind a desk. He stood up and introduced himself as 'Samuel'. Dave heard us and came out of his office to greet us.

"So are you installed in your new house? How do you like it?" I replied, "It's very nice, much better than we had imagined. And Inga helped us find things in the City." Margo remarked that the damage to the City was terrible. "And not only that," Dave added, "The loss of human lives was horrible. There were public executions each noon. Finally, the UNO dropped paratroopers to rescue the surviving 'Europeans'."

With that historical background, Dave led us around the building. As we entered a fairly large laboratory, Dave said, "Here is where we need your help, Margo. This the general chemistry laboratory." We saw a little room behind that was apparently used for the preparation of solutions. Dave than said, "Margo, your most important duty here will be to teach the two assistants how to make up the solutions, as well as to prepare various experiments for the lab."

Further down the hall, we were shown a much smaller laboratory where a young white man in a lab coat was setting up physical chemistry experiments. Dave said, "Hans, I have Margo and Jacques here to see the lab. Jacques is the new professor who will give the P. Chem. lectures and be in charge of the lab." Hans came forward to shake hands. He spoke excellent French, with a noticeable Germanic accent. As we continued down the hall, Dave mentioned that Hans was from a Protestant group in Germany and that he had a very good background in chemistry.

We then entered a room where there were several desks. Dave explained, "This the office for the Professors. I know that each should have his own, but we just can't do that here. You'll have to share. I hope you'll not be too inconvenienced." I replied with, "But of course, we are not looking for all the luxuries that we have known elsewhere." With a nod of understanding, Dave went on to say that we were now six professors to teach everything in math, physics and chemistry. He added, "Two of them have not yet arrived." Then, Dave went on to say, "We hope to start some of the classes next week. Would you be willing to start Monday?" We both agreed without hesitation. "Jack, if you could come Monday morning, I'll take you out to the 'paillote' to meet the students." I looked puzzled with Dave's reference to the paillote. "Oh, you'll see," he said. "I can schedule the class for ten, if that's OK with you. Perhaps, Margo you could come in at the same time to meet your two lab assistants and set up the first experiment. The two young men are hoping to become technicians. They are quite quick and should soon be able to take on much of the responsibility."

We both said that we would be in on Monday prepared to go to work. As we went out of the office we met a man, apparently of Asian origin. Dave presented him as, "Doctor Li, one of our two math teachers. Dave explained that 'Li' was both his first and his last name and that he had recently finished his Doctorate in Math in Lausanne, Switzerland." Li smiled, shook hands with each of us and addressed us in excellent French.

As we arrived back home, we were surprised to see a car parked in front of our house. It was the first car, aside from Inga's, that we had seen in the neighborhood. As we came up, a white lady got out and greeted us in English with a definite American accent. She said, "My name is Jane and I'm from Ohio. I'm happy to make your acquaintance, but my husband and I will be returning to the States tomorrow morning. I have brought you Vincent. He has worked for us for the last two years. He can do everything in the house and is completely trustworthy. Take him; you won't regret it." With that introduction Vincent got out of the car and came to shake hands. He was of average build, dark skinned and probably about forty years old. We agreed to take him on. In fluent

French, with a heavy accent, he said that he could start the next day, once "Missee et Madamee" were off to the airport. We understood his version of "Monsieur et Madame'.

Vincent very rapidly made himself indispensable. We found that, not only could he do all the housekeeping, washing, ironing, etc., but he was also an excellent cook. He explained that 'en temps Flamand', he had worked as a cook in a tourist guesthouse.

Each morning Vincent arrived early and immediately went to work picking up, washing dishes, making the bed and mopping the tile floors. He ate at noon with us, put the house in order and left at three in the afternoon. When our teaching duties began we were most happy that Vincent was there.

It was the following Monday morning when I had my first class. I met Dave as planned and he led me outside and into a circular enclosure with a thatched-roof. It was the paillote that Dave had referred to. It was open all around and furnished only with a blackboard on an easel. "So," said Dave, "This is your classroom!" As the students entered and found places to sit on the ground, Dave introduced me as 'Doctor Gilbert'. In all, I counted fourteen students.

THE MARKET

When Margo said that she would like to see the native market, Vincent immediately suggested that we go together. One morning when there were no classes we set off on a fairly long walk. Vincent carried a basket and I stuck the Parisian filet in my pocket. The market place was just a huge dirt field with many people sitting or squatting behind their items to sell. Here and there was an improvised 'stand' — a plank on a couple of rocks, for example. We saw two or three tables with meat displayed — only partially protected from the sun by some banana leaves and covered with flies. On a wire above each butcher's stand hung various sorts of game, wild birds, tiny antelopes — and in particular, small monkeys.

We asked Vincent about chicken. He replied by indicating the row of game. With a closer look I identified one of the poor creatures as a chicken. It had obviously run a long way. It was, to say the least, scrawny. We bought it anyway and put the llittle thing into the filet. We asked Vincent a lot of questions about the various, apparently edible items: "How do you prepare them? How much are they asking?" And, sometimes simply," What is that?"

At one point we saw a lady in the typical colorful wax. She was displaying a very large, almost flat basket on which were crawling little white worms. Vincent said, "No, they are not worms. They come from inside the trees. They are very good!" We learned later from our colleague Li that these little things are the larvae of the rhinoceros beetle. He had explained that they come from the interior of palm trees or bamboo and that they have different tastes depending on their origin.

While Vincent and the lady discussed the price, Margo and I exchanged looks and a couple of nods. Margo then said, "You can buy some for us, Vincent, if you promise to prepare them. We'll try anything once." The lady picked up a large banana leaf off the pile next to her. She made a cone and counted out the beasts as Vincent indicated. She then folded the leaf over the top of the cone and tied it all together with a string of raffia.

A bit further along in our promenade in the market, Vincent remarked, "If you would like me to fix the chicken following our tradition, you will need some peanut butter." Margo and I looked at each other in astonishment. "Well," Vincent said, "Here we often make the sauce with ground peanuts — and of course lots of pili-pili." With that, we stopped asking questions and just followed Vincent. He went to another lady who spooned out peanut butter, again on a banana leaf. And at yet another stop he bought a couple of bright red peppers — the pili-pili.

On the way out of the market, Vincent bought a basket full of green leaves. They were from the manioc tree, whose roots are used to make flour. On the way home, Vincent said, "Be careful of those little beasts in your sack. They will try to eat their way out." I looked down and, sure enough, there were already several holes in the big banana leaf that was their prison. We managed to get them home anyway.

Vincent immediately attacked the poor chicken, plucking it, decapitating it and cleaning out the interior. He than cut it up and tossed the pieces into a pot of boiling salted water. When the chicken finally got tender, he took the pieces out of the water and continued boiling the liquid until it was down to about half its volume. He dried the pieces of chicken and fried them very lightly in palm oil and made a sauce with the peanut butter, the broth and the pili-pili. I noticed that when he cut up the pili-pili he avoided touching it with his hands. He explained, "If you aren't careful and rub your eyes or touch any other delicate place, it will burn for a long time."

A bit later when we had left Vincent to work in the kitchen, we heard banging. We took a look and found him squatting in front of a big wooden mortar, pounding the manioc leaves with the pestle that our neighbor had given us. He cooked the product like spinach — but with the addition of palm oil. He said that you had to pound manioc leaves to break up the tough fibers.

To prepare the little beasts for the first course, Vincent heated a pan with some palm oil, threw in a couple of crushed cloves of garlic followed by the squirming 'worms'. They were quickly put out of their misery.

When Vincent called us to the table he announced that we would now be served in African style. He came to each of us with a bucket of warm water and a towel. We were to rinse our hands before eating. We noticed that there were no knives or forks on the table. Vincent then brought in the various dishes and introduced us to fou-fou. It was a warm, rather pasty dough made from manioc flour and water. As such, it had no taste at all, but dipped into the peanut sauce, it became very good. In fact, the only problem was the pili-pili. The sauce was like fire. The little beasts were lying peacefully on their bed of manioc leaves. They tasted very much like shrimp in the 'hot' sauce.

At the end of the meal Vincent came to each of us with a fresh bucket of hot water in which to wash our hands. We had drunk only water throughout the meal, but with the highly spiced dishes, we understood. Water, or perhaps beer, was the only beverage that was appropriate.

MISS MÉHARI

IT WAS JUST AFTER THE Fac had closed for the Christmas Vacation. Vincent arrived early in the morning, as usual. However, he was somewhat excited and immediately started talking about the drums. "Yes," he said, "Last night they had a message for you! They said that your things were on the boat from Kinshasa. All should be unloaded by now." "Oh, that's great," I said. "Let's go see."

Vincent showed us the way down to the river where the boat was docked. There she stood, 'Miss Méhari', along with our two footlockers. I presented my copy of the bill of lading and my identity papers and signed the receipt, as indicated by the agent. "Ok," I said, "Now let's see if I can start it." I got in and was surprised to see that the ignition key was still there. After much coughing and sputtering, she came to life and was running on both feet, as they say.

I got out and with Vincent's help got the two footlockers into the back of the car. Vincent crawled over the front seats and sat down on the board behind. Margo got in next to me; we pulled shut the two canvas doors and started off. In spite of some confusion about the gearshift, I was able to drive to our house. Both Margo and Vincent were like children with a new Christmas toy. I too played with the car, adjusting the idling and checking the oil, tires, etc.. I found a metal box of parts and hand tools bolted to the floor in back. I thought, "Good 'old' Michel back in Bobigny."

When I saw Dave the next day at the Fac I announced the arrival of the Méhari. "Now," he said, "You can see some of this magnificent country. When you have a morning free, drive up along the river to the falls at Wagenya. It's not far. There, the sight of the fishermen at work is worth some pictures.

So with Miss Méhari our first outing was to Wagenya. The Stanley Falls, as they were called, were very impressive — a tremendous rush of white water over which had been constructed a lattice-like structure of heavy timbers that traversed the rapids. It was literally crawling with dark, naked bodies that were scooping fish out of the water with wicker baskets. We were just taking a couple of pictures when an African man approached us along the shore. He looked out-of-place in his correct attire. He addressed us in English with, "Why are you taking pictures of those naked boys? They should be ashamed to be seen like that — and you too to be taking photographs." At first we were quite mystified by the man's remarks. Later, Margo and I discussed the incident. We felt that our critic well represented the unfortunate effect of the 'European' influence on local traditions. Why should either the young fishermen or us be ashamed? What was most interesting was the method of fishing, although it could hardly be described as efficient. It was clear to us that the gentleman in question had been 'educated' in a mission school. When I saw Dave a day or two later I told him about our interesting visit to Wagenya, although I refrained from telling him of the encounter with our critic.

Then David suggested that we might like to go to Yangambi to see the Lab there. He explained, "Before the Simba uprising there was a plan to develop an agricultural research center there. Unfortunately, it was all stopped and I don't know what the situation is now." I asked, "That could be very interesting, but where is it?" He replied, "It's a small town about thirty miles down the river. You could normally make it a nice day's outing. You do, however, have to cross the Lindi River. That can sometimes be difficult."

The next day at lunch I told Margo and Vincent what Dave had said. Margo responded with, "Oh let's go. That sounds like fun." I then asked Vincent, "And what do you think; would you like to go along?" "Oh yes, very much," he replied with excitement — but with some doubt in the expression on his face.

The following week we had a day with no teaching duties. So we planned the adventure. Vincent packed a picnic lunch and we set off early. We left Kisangani along a small road, one of only two. The other one went east. We very soon arrived at the Lindi River where it joins the Congo. We drove to a small dock and saw a ferry, as if it were awaiting our arrival. When I asked in French when the boat would leave, the attendant looked at me with total incomprehension. Vincent then discussed the question with him in Swahili and explained to us that there was no gas for the boat. The man there had said that if we could provide the gas, the boat would take us across the river.

In the box that Michel had provided there was of course several feet of plastic tubing. I asked myself, "How could he have thought of that?" We siphoned a beer-bottle full of gas from the tank and used it to get the boat underway.

On the other side of the river the road become even narrower, just wide enough for the car. It was lined with bamboo that at times joined above to create a tunnel. Suddenly, we arrived at a small village and, with no warning, a chicken ran right before us. It was impossible to stop the car soon enough. As we saw nobody around, we continued on our way to Yangambi.

As we approached the town, we saw more and more people walking along in the same direction. We soon understood that there was a big market, extending along both sides of the road. We stopped when we seemed to be in the town and Vincent got out to ask directions. After a few shrugs of shoulders he found someone who waved 'further on and to the right'. We pulled up in front of a low building. The remains of a sign in what had once been a lawn, indicated '......[unreadable].... Agriculture'. "This must be it," I remarked, "The research lab."

There was nobody in sight and no answer when we knocked on the door. So, we decided to eat our picnic. As we were finishing lunch, a man appeared and walked up to the entrance. We called to him and asked about the lab. I explained that we were from Kisangani and that my wife and I were teachers at the University. He shook hands with Margo and me, addressed us in French and greeted Vincent in Swahili: "Jambo, habari? Jina langu ni Robert." Then he said to us that his job was to guard the Laboratory, as there was no longer anyone working there. He asked if we would like to visit it anyway. I replied that we would like very much to see it.

We followed Robert into the building. I noticed that he carefully locked the door behind us. We entered several small labs that were equipped with instruments for analytical chemistry. In one of them I was surprised to see an infrared spectrometer — exactly the same model that I had left behind in Washington! I had the impression that it had never been used.

As we walked around the building, Robert told us the sad story of the Laboratory as a result of the Simba revolt. He said that the members of the Staff who were caught, were executed. His personal history was indeed sad. He said that he had escaped into the forest, but when he returned he found that his wife and children had all been killed. We left Robert, the Laboratory and Yangambi with the thoughts of what it must have been like at that period.

We pushed along the road as fast as we could. The problem was to arrive at the ferry before dark. When we came up to the village where we had had the encounter with the chicken, there were several people standing in the middle of the road waving us to stop. They said that we had to pay for the chicken that we had killed. We discussed the question through Vincent, who interpreted for us. He said that they were asking two zaïres, more than twice the market price. I agreed anyway, but asked if we could have the chicken we had bought. Vincent felt that it was a reasonable question, but that he was sure that by now the chicken had been eaten. He added that it was good that I had agreed to pay, as he was somewhat afraid that we too might have been eaten.

We arrived at the ferry just in time. Night 'fell' just as it docked on the other side of the Lindi. The relatively short ride back to Kisangani was uneventful. We returned to our teaching at the Fac with a better understanding of what the people had gone through during the occupation.

One day when I was downtown looking for someone to develop our pictures, I met two of my students. We started talking. Then they looked at each other — and then at me. One of them asked, "Would you like to join us for a glass?" I replied, "Yes, very much indeed." They led me into a café and we sat down at a little table. When they asked me what I would like to drink I replied, "A glass of beer would be perfect." The boys joined me and were overjoyed to learn that I was not a teetotaler.

The waiter came with the beer, along with a small dish of what appeared to be peanuts. "Oh, this is a special occasion," one of the boys remarked. "It is most certainly in your honor, Professor, that we are served the little appetizers." "Yes, but what are they," I asked? The boy replied, "Before we answer, just try them." He picked up a big pinch and munched away, as with peanuts. I did the same and found them to be salty, smoky and tasty. On of the boys then identified them as smoked termites. I had to admit that I found them to be quite good and was reminded of a picture I had seen in a National Geographic of a chimpanzee fishing termites out of a mound with a stick. However, they were neither smoked nor salted — just wiggly.

We chatted for quite a while. The students asked many questions about life in Europe and America. At one point they turned to science and asked me about the Nobel Prizes. I explained their origin and the procedure for choosing the laureates in the various fields. Then, one of the students remarked, "Professor Gilbert, you explained in one of your lectures that our knowledge of the liquid state was very limited and that there was a need for a model." "Yes, that's true," I replied. "They are neither like solids, where the molecules are more-less-frozen in place, nor gases, where they are considered to have random distributions in space and time." The student continued, "But, Professor, you do research don't you?" "Yes," I answered, "I've been working on the structure of crystalline solids and polymers." Then he asked, "But why don't you study liquids? You might get the Nobel prize." I was stopped by that one. 'Touché.'

I decided at that moment that once established in the Lab in Bordeaux, I was going to work on the 'structure' of liquids. I never forgot that discussion with my two students in Kisangani.

I was still thinking about it when we walked out into the sunshine. My students were very grateful, as I had picked up the bill. I knew that they couldn't afford to pay it.

VICTOR

IT WAS ALREADY INTO THE second semester. I was seated in the office when Dave came in with a big smile. "Hello, Jack, I have great news! Jérôme just called from Kinshasa. It was by our new telephone, not on the talking drums! Our new teacher has arrived. He will hopefully be on the plane this afternoon. We will finally be able to get the organic chem class started. By the way the new man is our very first African. I have been trying for some time now to hire one for our Staff, but they usually prefer to remain abroad after their graduate work."

"That is good news," I replied. "But how is he going to teach the whole year course in less than one semester?" "Well, I hope he's willing to play 'catch-up', Dave said with a laugh. "And the students, too," he added.

The next morning Dave called a little meeting to present Victor to his new colleagues. He was tall and dark-skinned — probably about thirty years old. Dave made a little speech in French, but remarked that like most of us he spoke excellent English and had recently finished his Ph.D. in the States. He went on to say that Victor was looking for a place to stay until a studio would be free at the Residence.

Later that morning I chatted with Victor a bit. He switched to English and remarked that he, like me, was somewhat more comfortable in it. He said that he had spent a number of years in Oregon, where he was a grad student at the University. I thought back to Bengt, my friend at the Research Center. When I asked Victor if by chance he had known him, he exclaimed, "Yes! He was in our living group, the 'Chowder House'3*, for several years." I told Victor of his disillusion with industrial research and his sad death. Victor responded, "I had heard that he had died, but I didn't know of the circumstances. How sad. He was a genius, you know."

Later I mentioned that we had a spare room and perhaps he would like to stay with us until he got his apartment. "That would be very nice," he said. "You are very kind." I had rather assumed that Margo would have no objection to my invitation. She didn't, of course.

One morning after my lecture in the paillote a student came up to chat. He was Mat, one of the two with whom I had had beer in town. "What have you seen of my country," he asked? He was amused when I replied with my description of the trip to Yangambi. "Would you like to see Kisangani 'by night', as they say?" My immediate reaction was, "Yes — and I'm sure that my lady would like that too."

That evening Victor was with us at dinner. I brought up the idea of 'going out' with the students. As I expected, Margo was enthusiastic. Victor said, "That would be very interesting, I'm sure. May I come along?"

The following Friday night we picked up the two boys as we had agreed. Mat joined Victor on the back seat and the other boy climbed behind and sat down on the toolbox. We then followed their directions to what was a run-down house. However, it had electricity, as evidenced by the string of colored light bulbs along the roof above the entrance. As we approached we heard music — old records being played on a system that was very much lacking in quality.

There was a bar along one wall of the room and a number of tables around a space for dancing. The barman came out to greet the boys, who were obviously regular customers. After we had been served our beers and had chatted a bit, Victor asked Margo if she would like to dance. She was beaming as he asked my permission. I replied, "Yes, of course. I don't know how." They appeared to have catalyzed a reaction, as several others got up to dance. There was one couple, as well as a number of women in their colorful dresses. Each of these ladies had a contrasting foulard pulled around her derrière and tied in front.

While Margo and Victor were preoccupied with dancing, the boys talked a bit about the customs of the country. Mat said, "The ladies here are called 'femmes libres'. That means that they are available for a price." 'Yes, I gathered that," I replied. Mat added, "The going price is a can of sardines; although an unusually attractive one may ask two." I withheld comment.

As we sat watching the passing scene, I noticed a white man sitting at the far end of the bar. He was alone and just sat there with his glass in front of him. I asked, "And what is the role of the man there at the end of the bar?" Mat lowered his voice and replied, "He's an American. He is with the CIA. You'll find one in every establishment in the area. They are here to observe — to be aware of everything that's going on."

Later on, each of the two boys danced once with Margo. Then they indicated that they would not be going back with us and went off to make other contacts. I hadn't noticed if they were provided with cans of sardines.

We learned later that there were several establishments of the same type in the area. We also found that there was a more sedate place that was the rendezvous for the 'mundele'. It was run by a Greek couple. It had soft music, served meals and was frequented almost exclusively by white people — the so-called 'Europeans'. The CIA agent was no doubt present, but he was more difficult to identify.

One day near the end of the semester I had a lab all afternoon. Margo came back from the Fac a bit earlier than usual. She found Victor sitting in one of the armchairs. She said hello and went back to change and to leave him to the preparation for his courses. Somewhat later, she returned. She was now just wrapped in the traditional 'wax'— just enough to hide what she had to offer. She came over and sat down next to him on the arm of the chair. Little-by-little, he relaxed — or was that the word? — and put down his papers. Then when she stroked his thighs and at last opened his shorts, she found an enormous erection. She cried out, "It's beautiful," when she saw his huge tan penis. She noticed that he had been circumcised following the African tradition.

He slid down in the chair as she straddled him and mounted over that magnificent object of her desire. He joined in, thrusting up energetically to enter her. Suddenly, at the crucial moment, he indicated that she should turn over. She put her head down on the carpet and presented her full derrière. He came down behind her and slowly entered again, as he pressed her cheeks together. He pushed on to the base of her sexuality with an intensity that she had never known before. She reached below to stroke her clitoris and came three times, as Victor continued. Her screaming orgasms were profound, magnificent — no other words to describe the ultimate — that was it. She had found her seventh heaven. Victor gave her his gift with a long groan of pleasure. They said nothing. Their mutual understanding was complete.

ACROSS AFRICA

THERE ARE MOMENTS WHEN I consider myself to be a 'slow learner'. True, I had noticed that Margo and I were having a personal relationship that seemed to be 'running down'. It was certainly not like what we had known back in DC. Perhaps it was that we were now always together and sometimes preoccupied with our work. And then there was the excitement of our rendezvous when Margo was my little student — perhaps because our relationship was forbidden. And yes, maybe because sex – yes, that's it —was now too easy to have. In any case it was apparent that there was a problem in our life as a couple.

I had finished correcting the final exams and had started to think about the return to France. Yes, that is where I was intending to go, as the post in Bordeaux was very attractive. It was a chance, perhaps my last, to get back into research as I had known it. As for Margo, it seemed to me reasonable that she would go back to start work on her thesis. Or?

I stood up to greet her as she came in. She appeared to be in a serious mood. When I approached her she said, "No, I just want to talk." I replied, "I'm not surprised. I have been thinking." She looked down and, although it was not visible, I had the impression she was blushing. "You know, Jack, I don't want to leave. I've found my roots here — emotionally, at least." "Sure," I said, "And perhaps that's not all." "Yes," she admitted, "You are quite right, as usual. I want to stay here with Victor." What could I say? "Of course I'm leaving to take the job in France and I will miss you terribly. Anyway, it was fun while it lasted." That night she came to me in bed for the last time. It was her way to say goodbye.

Early the next morning I finished packing the Méhari and hooked a 'vache' on the side of the hood. It was a canvas bag filled with drinking water. As I had learned, nobody would go off across Africa without a supply. The breeze as the car goes on cools the water, at least a bit relative to the ambient temperature. Before leaving I gave Vincent a mitabish. Margo had already given me mine the night before.

I took the road out of town toward the east. I had already planned to cross through Uganda and Kenya. I thought that from Nairobi it would be easier to return to Europe. In any case there was no passable road down to Kinshasa and I didn't want to wait for the unpredictable boat down the Congo.

The dirt road was narrow and soon lined with bamboo that sheltered it from the thick forest. It was hard to imagine that this was the only route across Central Africa. There was no sign of any other vehicle. From time-to-time a lady in the typical dress passed, usually with a heavy load of wood or bananas on her back. Near each little village a couple of men were often seen clearing the overgrowth on the road with their machetes. The men were often dressed in just a piece of wax in the form of a skirt. A bit further on into the jungle I noticed that the occasional woman was also so adorned.

Towards the end of the morning I approached Bawafsende, a small town that had at one time been the site of an important Mission. Dave had told me how the missionaries were executed there at the time of the revolt. As I passed, I saw an old car that had belonged to the Australian missionaries who had established a school there. Riddled with bullet holes, it had been left there in memory of those who were shot on the bank of the Lindi River.

As I left the village, I passed through the market and bought a few things for my little lunch. I continued in the afternoon through the Ituri forest. It was very dense. I passed several small villages that were apparently of the Bantu, the Negros of the region. Otherwise there was no apparent sign of life. And then, suddenly, in the distance I saw a tiny figure beside the road. When I arrived at the spot where I had seen him, there was no trace. It was my first distant view of a pygmy.

A few kilometers further on I saw a figure standing beside the road. He was apparently a Bantu, dressed in shorts and tee shirt, and barefooted like everybody else. He waved at me to stop. He addressed me in French and asked me if I could give him a lift. He got in the car and we started to talk a bit. He explained that he spoke French because he had studied in a local mission. He said that his family was mixed, as his mother's family was from the pygmies, the BaMbuti. I let him off after a nice chat and I was pleased to have had the chance to talk with someone from the forest.

From time-to-time there was a little break in the dense forest by a Bantu village. The pygmies, as I had learned, remained as much as possible in their camps in the forest.

At one of those spots along the road I saw a little house, built of bamboo and adobe, with banana leaves as roofing. A Negro man came down to the road and greeted me with a gesture of welcome. He said a few words in Swahili and indicated behind him, in front of the house, where I saw a doll-like figure. She was very small and dark skinned. She was completely nude, aside from white painting that followed very artistically the curves of her little body. The man explained, if I understood what he said, that she was being prepared for the wedding. I saw that beautiful figure and was immediately excited — my imagination was carried away. I thought, "I'm sure that with what I have in my pocket, I can have that little thing to take along with me. Probably," I continued, "But wait, Jacot, don't be stupid. What would happen later? You could not cross the boarder with her. And if you left her anywhere, she would be served up for the village feast the following day."

I waved goodbye to the man and continued on my lonely way across the Continent. However, I continued to think about that little body. Had she already undergone the 'preparation' for her marriage? It was, as I had learned, the clitoridectomy that was systematically performed in this area on young girls as they arrived at puberty. What a horrible thought! Why should they be deprived of the most important joy of life?

Near the end of the afternoon I saw a little sign with a red cross, indicating the missionary hospital that Dave had told me about. I turned up a little road and found a settlement, several houses and a larger building that was apparently a garage. One of the houses looked as if had just arrived from somewhere in the Middle West. In fact, as I learned later, it was the case. It had been flown in, piece-by-piece. I stopped in front of the house and went up to the door. As I tapped, the door opened and a lady appeared. When I said, "Bonjour, Madame," she responded in English with a very American accent, 'What's the matter; don't you speak English?" I apologized and explained (in English!) that it was only that French was the official language of the Country. She said, "Nobody speaks French around here."

In spite of her rather cool welcome she invited me in and described the establishment. She said that she was a doctor and her husband was an automobile mechanic. They were in this part of Africa to provide emergency service to the missionaries. As she said, "Sometimes, we give some medical care to 'the others'." When I explained that I was an American and a teacher, she indicated that I could eat something with them and stay over night. When her husband came in I could see that he was more at ease and definitely more friendly. The next morning they accepted money for some gas for poor Miss Méhari, but refused any payment for my stay.

Early the next morning I continued along the way east. Suddenly, the forest disappeared and it was a region of savanna. I arrived at an intersection with another road, the route to Beni. There, I saw an adobe house with a thatched roof. Across one wall, 'RESTAURANT' was written in chalk. It was close to noon, so I went in. An usually tall, probably more than seven feet, dark-skinned man greeted me in a mixture of Swahili, French and English. I thought, "He could make a fortune playing basket ball in the US." He offered me the 'plat de jour' for ten makuta — roughly ten cents. He said that I would have to provide a beverage if I wanted it, but that there was a stand just down the road where I could buy one. I went out and got a warm beer and a glass out of the car. Meat in a very spiced sauce was served with rice. It was a curry in the general sense of the word. The meat was said to be smoked antelope.

After lunch I continued along the road to Beni. On the right there was still the dense forest— on the left the savanna. There was still no sign of other vehicles on the road. I passed through the town of Beni and continued up towards the mountains that more-or-less defined the frontier with Uganda. As Miss Méhari climbed up the road, I looked down to the right toward Lake Edward. There, along the bank of the lake I saw a herd of elephants. It was the first time that I had seen them in the wild. They were playing like children in the water — spraying each other with water and having a great time.

On up the hill I arrived at a little structure on the right. There was a pole across the road. A man in a ragged uniform came out and asked for my papers. He seemed satisfied with what I presented, removed the pole and indicated that I could continue. I crossed over into what was apparently a no-mans land. I had been told that there was less danger here than along the other passage up north, where fighting continued. I went on my way for several miles without any signs of life. And then, night fell. I continued with no idea of where I was — although presumably approaching the Uganda boarder.

It was interminable. I couldn't imagine that there were miles of no-man's land between the two countries. Finally, I arrived at a small house and a stop sign next to the road. Inside the house I found an African seated behind a desk. He greeted me in English, "Good evening, Sir. Welcome to Uganda." He asked why I had come and where I was going. He looked at my passport and said that there was no problem, providing that I left the country within the next two days.

I continued on the road, the first paved road that Miss Méhari had enjoyed since she left France. Then, in the distance I saw approaching headlights. They came nearer and nearer. I slowed down as they continued to advance. Finally, I came to a stop, as did the car in front of me. We were nose-to-nose. A big, dark man came out towards me. He was grinning from ear-to-ear. He greeted me with, "Hey, Man, you are in Uganda. Over here we drive on the left!" I laughed too. Of course I should have thought about it. We chatted a bit and I asked him where I might stay for the night. He said just to continue to Fort Portal. There, he said I could find a hotel with no difficulty. I thanked him for the information and for his sense of humor.

I did indeed find a hotel. It was very simple, but quite adequate. The next morning I was served a very typical English breakfast and I continued on my way across Uganda.

In the distance I saw tall figure, standing like a statue, with a pole — a sort of cattle prod in one hand. As I approached I saw that he was indeed tall — certainly over seven feet. I thought back to the restaurant where

I had eaten the smoked antelope. The man back there must have come from this tribe, the Masai.

I continued on the road east. I crossed several military vehicles full of soldiers. This was the period of Idi Amin Dada and the military domination of the country. At one point a soldier at the side of the road waved me down. He asked if I had a camera. When I replied, "No Sir, I don't have one", he took a quick look at the interior of he car and nodded OK. He then explained: You know that there is a military camp just over the hill?" I found it amusing that he had volunteered this information, but when he waved me on, I did so. Before long I arrived at Kampala, a city apparently mostly occupied by natives — with occasional well-dressed Europeans.

At one point the road dipped down next to Lake Victoria, a vast expanse of water. Further along the route I was followed by elephants and ostriches, the two moving at very different speeds. From time-to-time the giraffes came to the road to peer down at us, as it was certainly Miss Méhari who attracted their attention.

Arriving finally at the boarder, my papers were checked. I had the impression that my arrival on the other side of the country had been recorded and transmitted to verify my departure within 48 hours.

The arrival in Kenya was without incident. When I showed my passport and said that I would be leaving from Nairobi for my return to Europe, there was only a nod of agreement. The officer, a black in an impeccable suit and tie, asked if I had an address in Nairobi. I gave him the address of one of my former students in Washington. He was of Indian origin, with his home in Nairobi. He had said to me long ago, "If ever you get to East Africa, please come to visit us. We would be so honored." I had kept it ever since in my wallet, the little slip of paper that he had given me with his address.

RANGA

I PUSHED ON IN THE HOPE of arriving in Nairobi before dark. However, at six o'clock night fell and I still had some distance to go. I entered the city late in the evening and stopped at what appeared to be a gas station. The attendant, apparently an Indian, looked at the address and said, "You should have no problem to find it. Just continue until you reach a big intersection. Turn left there and follow the house numbers." I thanked the man and went on. Just as he had said, I found the building with no difficulty. It was a small apartment house. I entered, went up to the first floor and tapped on the door marked 'Ranganathan'. The door opened and Ranga looked at me as if I were a ghost. I greeted him with, "Hello, Ranga, do you remember your old chemistry professor in Washington?" "How in the world did you ever find me," he asked?

He invited me in and introduced his wife, an attractive young lady in a bright yellow sari and the red dot on her forehead. She came to shake hands in the European manner. I said, "I am very pleased to meet you, Madame. Please excuse me for coming here so late in the evening. The road was longer than I had hoped." Ranga then said, "If you have left your things in the car, you'd better go right down and get them. They would certainly be stolen before long."

Ranga helped me bring my stuff up the stairs. He then asked if I had eaten. When I replied, "Well, no, not since lunch." He asked his wife to fix something and she went hurriedly off into the kitchen. Within a few minutes she served up an Indian meal. There was a curry, with rice of course, and a vegetable dish consisting of green beans and pieces of potato. The vegetables were even 'hotter' than what I had known in the Zaïre. The unleavened bread Ranga described as 'chappati'.

After dinner Ranga and I talked about what had happened since we were in Washington. He laughed when I explained my affaire with

Margo. He said that some of the students had guessed it.

When he asked about my plans I told him about the post in Bordeaux. "So now," I said, "I'm on my way back to France. Perhaps you can tell me where to get a plane ticket." "Sure," he replied. "Tomorrow morning I'll take you to a friend who works in a travel bureau. And now, you are probably tired. I'm sorry that we can't offer you a better place, but you are welcome to sleep here on the sofa."

The next morning I thanked Range's wife for the hospitality and Range joined me in the Méhari to see about the plane ticket. We drove a bit into the center of the city. The population appeared to be mostly Indian, with occasionally poorly dressed Africans and well-dressed Europeans.

We stopped in front of a small office building. Inside we found a travel bureau, with a young Indian sitting behind the desk. Range greeted him with the traditional Indian gesture, the hands palms together and a little bow. Range introduced me as his professor and explained that I wanted a one-way ticket to return to Paris. The agent said immediately that there was no problem and that there was a flight each evening.

I then turned to Ranga and said, "But wait, I have another problem. I have my little car. I am attached to her after our long trip together, but she must be sold before I leave." They both laughed at my description of the car and Range suggested that I reserve for the flight the next evening. He said, "That way I can take you tomorrow morning to someone who will handle the car deal."

The agent then suggested, "Ranga, why don't you take the professor over to Sharma's garage? He can make an estimate of the value of the car and we can probably arrange to pay for the plane ticket between us." He then said to me, "If you have to wait for money from abroad, it will certainly take several days." I started to understand how business matters were handled in the Indian 'mafia' in Nairobi.

On the way to the garage Ranga asked how much I had paid for the car. He seemed to think that I could get enough for it to cover the trip to Paris. And, in fact, Sharma, the garage mechanic, agreed, although he pointed out that Miss Méhari needed four new tires. He also indicated that she might be more difficult to resell because of the left-side steering wheel. Finally, the sale was arranged and Sharma said that he would transfer credit directly to the travel agent. He also suggested that I keep the car and come back to the garage the following evening. He would then accompany me to the airport and drive the car back. "So", said Ranga,

"Let's get something to eat."

We drove back into the center of the city and parked the car. As we walked along the sidewalk, I saw a stand with piles of what appeared to pastries. Ranga explained, "Those are the 'samosas' of India. You see the vendor has two kinds, with or without meat." I suggested that we buy some so I could taste them. He ordered a couple of each kind. The man immediately plunged them into a deep-fry bath that was waiting. He handed us two little wax-paper packets and we stopped to eat on the spot. They were of course hot. But when I took the first bite I found that 'hot' was indeed the word to describe the 'piquantness', but the little triangles were also very aromatic. We stopped in a small restaurant that appeared to specialize in 'carry out' food — Indian, of course — to complete the midday meal.

Ranga directed me back to his apartment and insisted that I stay overnight. His wife served up another varied meal. It seemed that that the vegetarians had found every conceivable way to prepare vegetables and eggs. Ranga explained that many people in India are vegetarians, but whether they eat eggs or not is questionable.

The next morning Ranga suggested, "Let me show you something of our country. We have very interesting parks here where you can see many animals in the wild." I accepted with pleasure and after breakfast we took off to see the Nairobi National Park. It was not far from the city. It did seem a bit strange to me that his wife was never invited to go out. I guessed that it was the custom.

We drove along a dirt road through the park. There were many different animals to be seen — elephants, ostriches and giraffes. They were already my friends. But here we saw lions. They appeared to be in complete liberty and contented. They were beautiful animals. We drove up on a hill and looking south I could just make out the snowcap of Mount Kilimanjaro. On the vast savanna below there were herds of zebras and antelopes. Altogether, it was a very memorable sight.

Late in the afternoon I dropped Ranga off at his apartment and said goodbye to his wife — with my thanks for her hospitality. I drove to the garage to pick up Sharma, then continued to the airport. I picked up the ticket that was waiting for me and checked my big suitcase. Sharma was sitting in the driver's seat (on the 'wrong' side, of course) when I came back to the car. I thanked him for his help and said 'adieu' to Miss Méhari.

Back in the terminal I took a look at my ticket. I noted that there was a stop in Cairo, with a change in plane. So, I was not surprised when, finally, the flight I was waiting for was announced for Cairo. On the plane I was served the standard 'meal' and paid for a tiny bottle of ersatz Bordeaux. Thus, I thought, I was preparing for my return to France.

IV

THE RETURN

I MANAGED TO SLEEP A BIT during the night and had just finished the morning coffee when the plane started to descend. From where I was sitting I could not see out. Too bad, I didn't even get a glimpse of the pyramids.

In the air terminal my passport was immediately confiscated and I was told to remain inside the terminal. There was a four-hour delay before the departure of the next flight. There was no chance to do any tourism. Finally, it was announced, an Airflot flight to London — with stops in Rome and Paris.

On board I found my seat and settled down for a long day's ride. In the front seat there were two African ladies, judging from their bright colored dresses. Then, two uniformed men came down the aisle. I noted Russian on their caps and gathered that they were Soviet pilots. They stopped where the ladies were seated and, in gruff English, ordered them out. The two pilots took their places with no further comment. I had to think of how Jérôme had gotten our places on the flight to Kisangani.

The day was long. The plane landed in Rome and once again I saw nothing of the city. We didn't have to get out of the plane, although we sat there for a long time. We took of and, finally, the descent on Paris, Charles-de-Gaulle was announced and I was coming back home.

Once through customs I took a taxi to the little hotel on Rue Madame. I felt lonely on arriving there. I suddenly missed Margo.

The next day I telephoned Marie. Janine answered and I heard her exclaim, "Marie, C'est Jacques à la ligne!" Then I heard her voice on the phone, "My dear friend, have you now come back to France?" "Yes," I responded, "It was quite an adventure." Marie continued, "Please come in and tell me all about it." "Of course," I answered. "Can I come this morning?" "Yes, please do, I want to hear about Africa and, in fact, I need your help." The last remark puzzled me, but I answered, "I'll be there right away."

When I arrived it was like returning to family after a long absence. Janine came running to greet me with four bises and Marie came out of her office. She took my hand and then, gave me a big hug and a little bise. I was quite moved by their welcome.

I followed Marie into her office and took a seat. In answer to several questions, I told her about my experience. She was very pleased that it had been an agreeable one. She asked about Margo. I hesitated. Then I explained, "Well, Margo didn't come back with me. She seems to have found her roots down there — as well as a handsome African." I must have looked a bit sad, as Marie consoled me with, "I think I understand. And to be quite honest, I'm not surprised. Don't worry. You will very soon solve your personal problems."

I could see Marie reminiscing, as she continued. "Many years ago, just before the war, I was engaged to be married to a charming young man. He was sent off to the front and never returned. I then decided to devote my life to science — to teaching and research. It has sometimes been a lonely existence, but I have tried to put personal problems aside." She added, with a little smile, "At least for the most part." I detected some mist in her eyes in spite of her effort to hide it.

"And now," she said, "I need your help. Here is the problem. There is an important meeting in Maryland in a couple of weeks. My colleague, Jean Brémond, has been invited to present his research work there. However, the pour man just had a mild heart attack. It's not considered to be serious, but his doctor says that he absolutely must not make the trip. Guess what I'm asking you to do." I looked unbelievingly at the lady, as I realized what she was proposing. "But I don't know anything about his work," I stammered. "Yes, of course," she replied. "But that really doesn't matter. He has prepared his notes and all his slides. And probably more important, you have the linguistic advantage."

"Well, maybe," I was definitely not convinced. However, I thought of all that Marie had done for me. I said to myself, "Jack, you can't refuse."

Marie said, "Don't worry, Jacques, you can do it. Also just now you have time. I know that you want to get down to Bordeaux to start setting up your research program, but there will be little going on before the end of the vacation period. Oh yes, all of your expenses for your trip to the US will be paid and Janine will arrange for your plane reservations."

I left Marie's office with a box of slides and a file folder of her colleague's notes. "So now," I thought, "I'll have to learn something." And back at the hotel I started reading the notes. The subject was more-or-less in my field, although I was not familiar with the experiments that I was supposed to explain. By the time I had read the notes a couple of times and gone through the series of thirty or so slides, I started to gain some confidence.

When I checked in with Janine a couple of days latter, she asked if I could leave the following week for 'America', as she called it. "Sure," I said, "Whenever you can arrange it." When I phoned the next day she said, "I have tickets waiting for you at Roissy for Wednesday. You should check in by nine. I have left the return 'open', as I wasn't sure when you wanted to come back." "Yes, of course," I answered, "No problem. I do want to spend a few days over there, as I left some things in storage that need to be shipped." Janine added, "Marie is in class for the moment, but she wants to know how you made out with the notes and slides. Is all OK?" "Yes, I guess so," I answered. But I had to chuckle with her 'OK' that had apparently slipped into the French language. She added, "Bon voyage, as they say in English, from Marie and me."

A VISIT TO AMERICA

EARLY WEDNESDAY MORNING I CHECKED out of the hotel and took a taxi. The flight to the US was routine and long. I was like any business man off to the US for ten days or so.

I saw a bit of Washington, DC, as the plane came into the Dulles airport. The terminal was immense and virtually empty. I had to wonder why it had all been built. And, the bus ride into downtown was interminable. It was still light, although it was now three AM Paris time, when I arrived after a short walk at the tourist home on C street. I was welcomed like the prodigal son, although it had been several years. The lady said, "Oh yes, we remember you. And, we heard that you went off to France!" I thought, "What a small town Washington is." I explained that I was back for about ten days and would like to stay there. She assured me that there was always a place, even in tourist season — which it was.

The next day I took the street car back up seventh street — but it was no longer a street car! It was now the ugly, smelly buses that made that trip north. The rails had been macadamed over, although the unkept neighbohoods along Georgeia avenue were still the same.

I entered the old chemistry building, passing between the Doric columns to the Departmental Office. Mrs. Jones got up to greet me and called Mr. Watkins. "Mr. Watkins, it's Dr. Gilbert who's back!"

Mr. Watkins came out to shake hands. He said that I had been missed and asked me about my adventures abroad. He added that Dr. Fillmore had resigned to take on a post in California. The new Head was one of my young colleagues. Mr. Watkins then talked a bit about what had happened since my departure. He returned to the murder of the young couple and made some comments.

"I may not remember all that happened way back when, but I'm quite convinced that it was not the little insane guy, the Wart, as we called him, who killed the young couple. When I went through all the paper cups after the thesis party, I never found the one that I had marked with an 'X' on the bottom."

"But what happened to it, the one that you had marked," I asked? He replied, "I think that it was next to the bodies and was picked up by the Police to get the finger prints. I have the impression that they never noticed that the cup was marked." "But then," I asked, "Who was guilty of the murder?" "I'm sure," he replied, "That it was Rick, Rita's husband. He certainly had no intention of killing his wife. He slipped the cyanide into the cup and presented it to Jim because he had learned of his wife's affaire. He had no idea that she would be going down to share the drink with Jim. Of course he reused the cup that had the Wart's fingerprints. It was the perfect crime."

"Yes, I remember that Rita had said that she was going home," I replied. "But what happened to Rick?" Well, he left the Department immediately after the Wart was arrested and went off to New York. The last we heard of him was that he died from a drug overdose. He never forgave himself for his wife's death." And finally, I asked, "What happened to the Wart?" "Oh him, well, he was considered to be unfit to stand trial and was sent off to St. Elizabeth's. He was judged to be hopelessly schizophrenic. There's been no word from him since."

I said goodbye to Mr. Watkins and went back downtown. The next day I took a taxi to University Park and registered for the meeting. During the several days there I saw a number of my scientific colleagues from various parts of the World. On the afternoon of the third day it was my turn to speak — or rather for Jean Brémond. I introduced myself as his replacement and explained why he was unable to come.

I gave my well-prepared lecture. I felt that I had done a good job in spite of my lack of familiarity with the subject. At the end there was a serious applause. Then I called for questions. The first was from a young person who asked something quite general about the subject. I had no problem with a satisfactory, and somewhat pedagogic, response. Then and older man in the front row, whom I recognized as one of the well known spectroscopists, posed a question which I was completely at a loss to answer. After my hesitation and a brief response, I saw several smiles, a couple of headshakes in the audience and I understood that I had missed the point. I responded simply with, "I'm sorry, but I tried." I got another round of applause for my effort. After the banquet and the closing ceremonies, I took the plane the next day for my return to France.

BACK TO FRANCE

ONCE AGAIN IN MY LITTLE hotel on Rue Madame, I continued my autoreflection. Where am I now? What can the future bring? There were moments when I wished that the bed were not so cold. Maybe the best thing for me was to get back to work. I did miss my research lab.

When I called Marie the next morning, she asked me about my talk at the meeting in the US. I explained that, aside from one question at the end, it went well and I felt that I had presented Jean Brémond's work as best I could. She thanked me again for my help.

I responded with, "I was honored to do it for him — and for you. Now I want very much to go off to Bordeaux to organize for the following semester." She replied, "But of course, and I wish you courage and all the luck. Just a reminder: The lab down there will be more-or-less closed. You should probably contact James Lesquin at the Fac to be sure that you have access during August."

After a call to James I left Paris the following day. The return to Bordeaux was a replay of my first trip. Once again I was impressed by the countryside and more generally, by the agriculture of this immense farmland.

I returned to the little hotel on the Cours de la Libération in Talence. I was greeted on the terrace in front of the restaurant by the 'Patron'. He welcomed me with, "You have returned, the Canadian!" I didn't correct him, as it was always assumed that if I were American, I couldn't speak a word of French. I left my suitcase and took a room. I told him that I would like to stay until I found a suitable apartment.

A short block down the way I arrived at the entrance to the Fac and stopped at the little house just inside the gate. When I presented myself as the new professor. I was immediately welcomed by the concierge, who handed me the keys to the building and the research lab. There was also a note from James. He said that he would be in the following day and to make myself at home. With that encouragement I did so. I had the impression that all was disserted for the 'grandes vacances'.

On the top floor of the research building I walked down the hall and saw that James was now officially in charge. The door to what was Professor Robin's office was now adorned with a sign, "James LESQUIN, Directeur". And what a big surprise! The next door down the hall displayed, 'Professeur Jacques GILBERT'. What could be a more elegant welcome to my new corner of the scientific world?"

My little office was ready for my arrival. Aside from the desk and chairs, there was a big bookcase — just awaiting to be filled with my collection of scientific volumes. Best of all was the view over the Campus, with the Château Haut Brion, and the vineyards off in the distance.

The next morning I came out of the hotel and crossed the street to an épicerie. I bought a few supplies and noticed a bulletin board with many items to rent or sell. When I saw that there was an apartment for rent in the area I wrote down the address. I asked the lady how to find the apartment. She replied, "Oh that's very easy. You go up the Cours past the Fac. You'll pass a garage and just a bit further you'll see the post office across the street. Turn right and continue along the same sidewalk and you'll see the apartment building."

With those very specific directions I found the building with no difficulty. I met the concierge. She showed me immediately to a one-bedroom apartment on the first floor — that is, just upstairs. It might have been described as 'partly furnished', but with certainly all I would need for the present. I found the price reasonable and agreed to rent the apartment. But when I explained that I was the new professor at the Fac, she seemed quite flustered and said that it was such a great honor that I would be her 'guest'.

I walked back down to the Fac and noticed that the garage was identified by the Citroën emblem. I said to myself, "I'll come back here later to see if I can find a car of some kind." I arrived at the Lab just as James was coming in. He greeted me with a warm welcome to the 'Sud Ouest'. We sat down in his new office and for two hours discussed our research plans. He was somewhat familiar with my work on the spectra of polymers and crystals. However, I went on to describe what one of my African students had remarked about the structure of liquids. I said, "And so, I now want to start a project on the liquid state. Although the spectra are relatively easy to obtain, the major problem is that there is no model upon which to base their interpretation. I hope to tackle the theoretical side of this question right away."

As the new director of the Laboratory, James laid out his program and promised to give me as much help as possible. He indicated that he could provide me with an interesting budget, as well the aid from the personnel of the Lab. He said that he hoped to have several new graduate students in September, as well as a new secretary.

James went on to talk of the region, the Aquitaine, and the many things to see and do. He pointed out that as one went in each direction there were marvelous attractions. I explained that I hoped to have a car so that I could travel a bit during the August break. 'Yes," he exclaimed, "You must go to the Coast, to Arcachon and down through Les Landes to the Spanish boarder. And while you are down south go up into the mountains to visit the Basque villages. And there is the interior, the region of the Dordogne and Bergerac, as well as the north to La Rochelle and the islands nearby." With great enthusiasm he presented his Cook's tour of his beloved part of France.

As we were leaving, he said that he would be going with his family to Aix-en-Provence, "Another beautiful region of France. My wife comes from there," he added. We shook hands and exchanged 'Bonnes vacances'.

After lunch at my little hotel I walked back up the Cours to the garage that I had passed earlier. The mechanic in his grease-stained blues came out with, "Bonjour, Monsieur le Professeur," and a handshake. "But how did he know who I was?" He explained, "I just had lunch with my mother and she told me of your arrival. She is the concierge in the apartment building where you just rented." I laughed and responded, "It is indeed like a small town here."

When I told the mechanic that I wanted to buy a used car, he started by showing me several high-class models. I said, "Well, they are very nice, but I really want something much more ordinary. In fact I just sold my

Méhari when I left Africa." He seemed surprised, but then changed his presentation as we went further back into the garage. I hesitated when we passed a 'Dianne', but further on I saw a Méheri! "How much would I have to pay for her," I asked? He quoted me the asking price, but when I indicated that it was more than I wanted to pay, he said that he would contact the owner.

When I came by the next day the mechanic said that the price had been reduced. I accepted the offer. And thus it was that I was now the owner of 'Miss Méhari II'. Over the next month we traveled throughout the region. Between trips I concentrated on the study of the liquid state. Fortunately, I had access to the library in the Lab, where I found many references. They were often difficult to understand.

From time-to-time Miss (Méhari II) and I went off on little trips, but I often wished that we had another companion. First we went off to Arcachon; it was the season. As we came into the city I saw a low wall between the road and the beach. We stopped to take a look and saw that we had found the so-called 'topless beach'. "Strange," I thought that people here were so concerned about such things. After a year in Central Africa I could only consider the attire — or lack thereof — as normal.

One morning after a night in a little hotel at Le Moullau, just south of Arcachon, I came down to the terrace where there were a number of tourists. They were eating oysters, raw of course, as I had known in New England. I ordered the same, with a bottle of dry white wine. It was unusual at that hour of the morning, but excellent anyway — as a brunch?

I left Le Moullau in the bright sunshine and headed south. In the pine forest just behind the great dune of Pyla I left Miss and started up the sandy slope. I had certainly underestimated the effort involved to climb this impressive pile of sand. At the top I enjoyed the magnificent view over the bay of Arcachon and Cap Ferret in the distance. Below in the intensie heat of the sun, focused by the curveture of the surronding sand, there was an assortment of bronzing bodies of all shapes and sizes. I went back down with these imiges and rejoind Miss for the return to Bordeaux.

KRISTINA

With the end of the 'grandes vacances' the Lab was suddenly occupied. I made the acquaintance of the Staff, several of whom I had met on my previous visit. James introduced a technician, Jean-Pierre, whom he described as the specialist with the new Raman instrument. At the tea session that afternoon everybody talked about the vacations. Once the recent ones were described, the subject turned to the forthcoming Christmas vacation — and then we have the ski vacation in February! Maybe I was too serious, as my thoughts were on my research.

The next morning there was a group at the entrance to the main office. James was there to present the new secretary, Mlle. Cassel. She stood up, tall and thin, in a bright green dress. She had blond hair that fell to her shoulders. All together she was a most beautiful young lady. She came to shake hands and introduced herself as Kristina. I could see that I was not the only one there who was impressed by her looks. I had the impression that a couple of the younger ladies on the staff cinsidered her to be serious competition. I remarked, "Perhaps you are of Swedish origin." "But yes," she replied, "How did you know?" "I thought that it was obvious from your looks," I answered.

Over the next several days I noticed that the office was very often occupied by male visitors. I, too, found excuses to talk to Kristina and finally, one day, I got up enough courage to ask her out to lunch. We walked out through the big gate and down to the little restaurant that I knew well. The 'Patron' came to shake hands with me and was obviously impressed when I presented Kristina.

After a simple, but good, meal and coffee we walked back up to the Campus. Every male and many female passersby turned to take a look at my companion. I felt the usual male reaction of pride in my choice. There was no question; she was absolutely gorgeous.

During the next few weeks we often had lunch together. Then, with the beginning of the concert season in Bordeaux, we went to the 'Grand Théatre' in the center of Bordeaux. All was played 'cool' until the day when I invited Kristina to have lunch with me the following day in my little apartment. When she accepted with a smile, I went immediately to the preparation of a little meal. I looked up typically Swedish receipts and settled on Gravad Lax. I went down to the Marché des Capucins near the Place de la Victoire. I bought fresh salmon and spinach, and with some difficulty was able to find sprigs of fresh dill. For the last I had had to look up the word in my dictionary. I had found it: 'aneth'. I went back home and followed to the letter the directions for the preparation. On the way back I picked up a bottle of Champagne — hardly a Swedish specialty, but she said she adored it! It was at room temperature, so I put it in the refrigerator. Then, there was the apartment. I tried to think of everything to put it in order — impossible, of course.

The next morning I was not in my usual calm state. It was not really panic, but I was nevertheless excited. I peeled the potatoes and put them into cold water. Perhaps, after Kristina's arrival, I could find twenty-five minutes to cook them. I went off to the Fac with little interest in science just then.

When I came out of my office I met Kristina. It was not yet noon — just a bit early! We walked rather hurriedly to the apartment. Somehow I remembered to put the fire under the potatoes, but that is not where it was. I put the Champagne in the freezer section of the refrigerator to 'frappé', but my thoughts were elsewhere. I had forgotten for so long the greatest pleasure of life.

We then enjoyed the second one. Kristina apparently appreciated my culinary efforts. But when I took the Champagne out I found that it was already partly frozen! — a 'grosse mistake' on my part. However, in the following weeks she came often for our joy of being together. We also went out on weekend excursions following James' suggestions.

And so it was one day that we were in bed, in each other's arms, after a most intense and mutually satisfying experience. In that relaxed moment my curiosity prompted me. "Tell me, Kristina, how you got here in France; you said that you were born in Sweden". "Yes, but it's a very long story", she replied. I said, "Please tell it — there's no hurry — I want to hear it all." So, she continued.

"Papa was nineteen years old when he was called up for military service. At a young age he had shown that he was very talented in both music and art. The war had just broken out and he was rushed off to the front. The German advance was very rapid, so he was quickly captured and held in a camp as a prisoner of war. He was soon sent north to work on a farm — and much later to a port on the Baltic Sea. There he worked for some time as a docker."

"There, it was rumored that prisoners escaped from time-to-time on outgoing ships. So, one night Papa boarded one and went down into the hold. He crawled over the coal and finally dug a niche in a far corner. Early the next morning he heard the motor start up and soon the ship was underway — destination unknown to him."

"But that's an incredible story; how did he have the courage to do that," I asked? "I really don't know and can't even imagine, "Kristina replied," But he did it For Papa, it was far from comfortable in that corner of the hold, but then he had no choice. He knew that if he were caught, he would be shot." Time went by — for three days and nights he was barely able to move and had no food or water. Worst of all was his intense thirst."

"Finally, the boat stopped. Papa crawled out of his hiding place and peeked out from under the hatch. He saw boots and heard German. No way. He went back down and a few hours later took another look outside. There were no more boots and the men were speaking another language — one that he didn't understand. So he ventured out. He was immediately taken into custody and explained in English that he was a French citizen. He then learned that he was in the port of Stockholm. Sweden was neutral during the war, so Papa was turned over to the French Embassy. There he received a much needed bath, new clothes, and, little by little, food and water. He was saved."

"Papa was lodged in the Grand Hotel in Stockholm, where he recovered from his ordeal. He was then invited to a big banquet at the French Embassy, and was welcomed by the whole staff, including the

French Ambassador."

"The Embassy also helped Papa to find a few odd jobs. At first he was handicapped by the language. His English was quite good, but he soon found that it was not true that everybody in Sweden spoke English. Many of the younger generation did, but it was not at all general, and is not even now. However, with his knowledge of English and German, Papa was soon able to communicate in Swedish. After many odd jobs, he went into industrial drawing, where he had already some experience, as well as talent. He eventually found a good job as a draftsman in a small town a hundred miles or so north of Stockholm."

"It was there in the region of Avesta that he met a sweet sixteen-year-old, Monika. As a young, handsome man, with a charming French accent, she found him irresistible. As the end of the war approached, Papa made contact with his parents back in the North of France. He decided to return to see them. By the time the war had finally ended and he had planned his trip, it was evident that Monika was several months pregnant. Nevertheless, he made the long voyage back home. Although she had confidence, her girl friends laughed at her and insisted that she would never see her Frenchman again. However, he came back and was there for the belated wedding in a little Lutheran church and the birth of Kristina. Yes, it was like that that I arrived in the world."

"The young family stayed there in Sweden for three years while they considered the future. And then, they decided — they moved to France. It was a very difficult adjustment for my mother, as France was then suffering terribly from the war. Compared with Sweden, it was a primitive country. My poor young mother had no conveniences, as the toilet was out back and water came from a pump behind the house. What a change from what she had known in Sweden! And there was the linguistic problem, as she didn't know a word of French. "But, I was soon able to help. When I went to school at age three I became immediately at ease in French and so my mother progressed. As you know, children are quick to learn. Fortunately my father found a good job as a draftsman and the family situation became less difficult."

Kristina finished her reminiscences. "And now you know the story of my family." I had to think it over a bit, as I found it to be overpowering.

I reflected — and finally responded, "You know, you should write it up, as it has the makings of a great novel." "Perhaps", she said, "But it is only family history."

After a bit I expressed my thoughts. "Kristina, I would much like to meet my future mother-in-law — and your father too. Do you understand?" "Oh, yes I do", she cried!

ENDNOTES

1* The name of the country was changed back to 'République Démocratique du Congo' in 1987.

2* A somewhat vulgar name for a 'Vespasienne', a public urinal.. After the Roman Emperor, Titus Flavius Vespasien (69 – 79).

3* A student living establishment in Oregon. See, George Turrell, "The Light-Blue Scarf", Trafford Publishing, 2005.